SUGAR DOLL

SUGAR DOLL

JOHN B. THOMPSON

CUTTING EDGE

ISBN-13: 978-1-957868-38-7

Published by
Cutting Edge Books
PO Box 8212
Calabasas, CA 91372
www.cuttingedgebooks.com

CHAPTER ONE

Antoinette de Lage Salton stared into the cold merciless gullet of the pistol with numb fascination. Her palms were dank with sweat from the hysterical force with which she gripped the weapon. The muzzle leered at her, every tiny detail appearing to her staring eyes in etched clarity. Her pulses hammered thunderously in her ears and a tight suffocating weight lay heavy in her chest. She gazed at the shining serpentine bands as they wound their way from the depths of the barrel, stopping at the muzzle like long deformed teeth through which death would spit when she pressed the trigger. "Everything will be over ... everything will be settled ... everything will be all right ...." It seemed as though the gun was speaking to her but she knew it to be the thudding of her own thoughts.

Suddenly, with a spasm of revulsion, she hurled the gun from her with a frenzied motion, backing away as though from a poisonous reptile. The gun almost struck Granny Rosa who came through the door as Antoinette threw the weapon. Granny was about as wide as she was tall, her face smooth and virtually devoid of wrinkles, with eyes keen and wise.

She halted, favored Antoinette with the briefest of glances, then waddled over to the bed and dropped the load of sheets she was carrying. She turned and faced the girl.

"Whut you doin' chunkin' dat gun 'roun' like a tater? You might nigh struck me."

The girl seemed not to have heard her and she continued to stare with a trance-like fixation at the gun as it lay on the

1

floor. With a powerful sweep of her arms Granny hurled a chair behind Antoinette, striking her at the knees and precipitating her roughly into a sitting position. Granny pulled up another chair and sat.

"Now, den, Toni, you can tell you Granny bout it. Ain't I riz you frum a li'l bitsy ole baby, all the way …."

Antoinette broke the chains of her fear with an almost audible sound and fell against the old woman's breast with a sobbing cry of relief. She cried long and stormily, gradually subsiding into jerking sobs. She could smell the clean starched odor of the old woman's clothes, shot through with the friendly pungent aroma of plug cut tobacco and a well seasoned stone pipe.

"Come on, now," prompted Granny, "and tell me all about it."

A cry came from the girl's throat that made Granny wince. "Why … why … why did it have to happen to me?"

Granny rubbed the back of her hand against her nose. "How come *what* happen?"

The girl sat up straight and dashed the tears from her eyes. "Granny Rosa, I'm way over time …!"

Granny chuckled. "Shucks, you had me mos' skeered t' death. Lotsa gals you' age had dat happen, 'specially if you been playing 'roun. …"

Antoinette grasped the old woman by the arms with such strength that Granny gasped. "I haven't, I haven't, I tell you! I didn't play around, Granny. I was … *forced!*" Another hard sob shook her and her head sank in abject misery. Her voice was the wail of a lost child. "Oh, God, Granny! What am I going to *do?*"

"Rat now," snarled Granny, bouncing to her feet, "us goin' tell de boss and us goin' have a lynchin' roun' hyar … atter you tells me who done it."

Antoinette's silence stung the old woman into action.

She lifted the girl from the chair by main force and said, "You tells me, or I slaps hit outen you." Her voice was hard and uncompromising, reflecting the iron discipline which was Granny's toward both black and white who were in her charge.

The girl began to weep bitterly. "That's the trouble. I don't know. It was at night and I never saw him. I just waited and hoped I'd never have to tell …."

Granny sat suddenly. "Jesus," she breathed faintly. "Us is in a fix." She sat and thought for a minute, then she motioned with her hand. "Set down," she commanded, "and you can tell me all 'bout it frum start to finish."

The girl closed her eyes tightly and struggled against nausea for a moment, then nodded, "I'll tell you …."

The night was humid and muggy. Not a breath of air moved the leaves of the giant magnolia outside her upstairs window but the heavy perfume of the blossoms weighed her down like thick strangling webs. In the east, across Big Buff Creek, lightning flared and flickered along the horizon, showing the serrated teeth of tall pines. She lay in bed and tossed, partly because of the heat and partly because she had been getting a lot of sleep lately and her young pliant body was demanding activity. Thunder, muted and ominous in timbre, muttered fitfully in the distance between periods of heavy silence. Insects and frogs were silently awaiting the onslaught of the storm.

She got out of bed and stood in an open window, trying to catch a bit of air, but it was as tepid as that around the big bed, so she just stood watching the play of electricity, wishing the wind and rain would come.

She went to the bathroom and found a towel that would reach from her chin to the floor and mopped her face and neck. On an impulse, she ran water over it and wrung it out, and slipping her thin gown over her head, sponged her body, gasping delightedly at the cool rough touch, prickles of pure sensual ecstasy coursing over her. She scrubbed her back and thighs thoroughly, then her stomach and sharply erect breasts, touching them with careful pride, smiling to herself as their pink tips became taut and hard.

She sat on the window sill and draped the towel over her from chin to knees, tucking it close to afford the maximum benefit. Soon it was warm and she shook it out to cool, the air seeming hotter than ever. Again she ran the towel over her body, wishing it were not so much trouble to wet it again. She decided against it and draped it across her stomach, chest and shoulders.

The thunder had risen from a low growl to the sharp crackling explosions of field guns and a lone bolt of lightning tore a sprawling jagged crack across the sky. Immediately there was a rolling cannonade which almost split her eardrums—that one had been close. She fancied she could smell the sharp odor of ozone, where the bolt had seared the atmosphere, and her nose wrinkled appreciatively. Another bolt blazed across her vision like the forked tongue of some giant serpent, and again the window-rattling explosion and the long echoing roll. A little breeze sprang up and got stronger gust by gust.

Toni loved storms with all their prodigal waste of wind, water and electricity. Everything seemed cleaner and refreshed when they were done and the extravagant spendor of their displays delighted her. She pulled herself up in the window, a slim but marvelously curved silhouette in the violet spasms of light, her misty blond hair waving softly in the wind which now had mounted to gusty violence. She touched the cool skin on the under side of her thighs and on her arms, then thrust her hands under the mass of her hair, shaking it out to the full force of the wind. It whipped about, stinging her back and cheeks as the gusts played toss with it.

The first drop of rain was as big as a twenty-five cent piece and struck her slightly rounded stomach near the navel depression. She flinched and shuddered a little. Another followed, striking the valley between her breasts and trickled down to join the other. Then with a roar, the deluge came down. Toni stood on the roof outside her window and, holding her head inside, let the chill water sting her shoulders, back and legs. Like an acrobat, she arched her body, let her stomach catch its share then with a serpentine twist leaped back into the room and punished her tingling skin with a rough dry bath towel.

Invigorated and relaxed, she climbed naked in bed and lay spread-eagled on top of the cover, cool and comfortable. Outside, the storm fretted itself out in a final burst of rain and colorful electric display. The wind settled down to a cool steady zephyr, covering the girl's naked body with soothing caresses. She slept with the distorted flexibility of a kitten, her fine hair tousled and wild over her pillow, one arm across the smooth expanse of her stomach, the other outstretched toward the edge of the bed. One leg was extended straight out in front of her, the other drawn up, making a figure four. The lightning had ceased and the thunder was out of breath. Only the drip, drip from the eaves of the house and the ecstatic glee club efforts of thousands of toads disturbed the purple silence.

Toni slept on in the untroubled relaxation of youth and perfect health, her breath regular and calm. Her door opened slowly. In the inky blackness she would not have been able to see the intruder, even if she had been awake. The shadowy figure crept closer on carefully placed feet and stood above her. There was the sound of the rasp of cloth like the belt of a bathrobe being carefully untied, followed by a slithery gasp as though a bathrobe was being dropped to the floor.

Toni slept peacefully on and not until a heavy body landed upon her, did she awaken, her scream stopped by the palm of a hard hand. Her legs snapped instinctively together, but it was too late. Her strong young body arched and writhed with all the mad strength of terror, but the weight was too much. The cold sweat of numb freezing horror stood out in droplets and her partially pinioned hands gripped and clawed at the arms and shoulders above her, trying to reach his face and eyes but falling short.

Her legs strained and clenched with despairing strength but the efforts only weakened her further. She tried to bite the hand that was crushed over her mouth with such brutal force, but her teeth slipped off the tough palmar hide without being able to get purchase. Suddenly a sensation shot through her, and with another attempt to scream, she fought with renewed vigor but her strength was gone and it was only a brief hysterical spasm. The sensation went from a mere impression into a blinding wave of red raw agony which shot through her stomach and upward like a wave of wet fire and she fainted ....

"You see," she screamed, "I told you ... I don't know ... I never will know ... I ... oh, God!" A hard convulsive shudder shook her body, and her breath straining through set teeth bore droplets of froth.

Granny Rosa, pain and helplessness cutting a relief map of ridges in her face, slapped the girl a sharp blow across the face. Toni's cries became silent and sobs, hard and shaking, took their place.

Lavender Salton was taking her beauty nap. One might have said, without being too unkind, that she needed it. When taking a nap hers resembled no skin ever seen in its natural state reposing beneath layers of various unguents designed to feed starved tissue and to strengthen sagging muscles. She wore, in addition to the creams, a device which was supposed to avoid "gobbler's neck" or the wattle that comes with middle age.

Her figure was slight and delicate like the lines and skin of her face. There were no bovine traits in the Patterstall line she would say at the slightest or no provocation. She considered her skinniness sylph-like, and her starveling breasts as further evidence that there hadn't been a bull or cow on her family tree for three thousand years.

For her figure, for her aura of culture, and for the generally nebulous background which she made the most of she was an envied member of the Literary Club, The Daughters for the Preservation of Southern Culture and other such.

Lavender was not Southern, she was Boston, and she always contrived to picture Boston as suffering considerably by virtue of her absence from its august environs. Her sighs for Beacon Hill and Back Bay were echoed by the culturally undernourished, one and all, save those who had been there and had come away callously unimpressed just as some people can visit Richmond, Virginia, without suffering from anything save the inhabitants' stuffiness. With those who had visited Boston Lavender was delightfully vague as to just where she had lived or how long. This was because she had been there only twice in her life, once at the age of three.

She sat up in bed, after having been awakened, with a vigor that was both uncomfortable and unnecessary. "Rosa, how many times do I have to tell you not to awaken me when I'm taking my nap? If I've told you once I've told you a thousand times that when …."

"I come to ax you wheh de Boss is," said Granny breaking in on what she had learned might be a marathon of complaint.

"I'm certain I don't know. There are things which I have striven might and main to place on something like routine around here, and to date I seem to have reaped a veritable bumper crop in exactly the opposite direction. What has happened that should make his presence so terribly important as to …." She stopped. Not even Lavender enjoyed talking to a closed door.

Jefferson Salton's face twitched alarmingly and he rubbed it hard with his long sensitive fingers. "Now come over that again, Granny, and do it slowly. I'm afraid you lost me somewhere …."

"I sed she done got bigged. Dat otta be plain enuff fer you. Some low bastud done ravished her in her bed and hit was dahk and she couldn't see who hit was. Now she in a fambly way, and whut us gon' do 'bout it?"

He sat suddenly in a handy chair and held his face with both hands. He had had a certain trying scene with Lavender last evening and today his usual quart had disappeared immediately after dinner. Since then another quart had gone the way of its predecessor. He wasn't drunk but he had trouble focusing his mind.

"Where is she now?"

"She in her room sleepin'. Dat's wheh I lef' her bout a hour ago."

"Who do you think it could have been, Granny?"

"I ain't got no ideer. All I know is, my Sugar Doll is in a passel o' trouble and up till now, she done allus come to me and I been able to do somethin'. Dis here thaing done got me and I can't think o' nothing." The old woman began to sob, tears trickling down her fat cheeks.

Jeff sat silent for a while, his gaze flitting aimlessly across the broad, tree-dotted lawn. Tremendous columns narrowing the view, making him unconsciously frame the landscape between them, blocked his vision on either side.

Granny Rosa sat on the porch steps and wiped her eyes on her apron. "Fust time she ever come to me fer sumpn' and I couldn't tell her whut to do. I operated on a white gal onct a long time ago and she likened to died. I ain't never tetched another one since and I ain't gon' touch my Sugar Doll neither. Peoples can set back and make all sortsa rules fer other peoples but I ain't never seen *dem* ackin' so sweet. Now mah Doll done hadda mislick and us can't do nuthin'."

A slim blue convertible flashed around the driveway on the east side of the house and disappeared in a swirl of dust. Salton shook his head. "There she goes," he said sadly, "I wonder what she intends to do?"

"Well," rasped Granny, standing and glaring at him, "I come in her room rat after dinner jes' in time to stop her frum killing herself wid you' pistol." With that, she left him still sunk in his chair, trying to make his sulky brain function.

Lavender came out on the porch and sat near him. "I can't tell you how sorry I am," she said softly. "What a terrible thing to happen to you! What a blow it must be! I am awfully sorry, but I must say, I'm not terribly surprised."

He faced her slowly. His usually mild brown eyes were flaming and held mad glints. "A terrible thing to happen to *me?*" The muscles controlling the corners of his sensitive mouth were leaping spasmodically unnoticed. "What do you think it is to her—or don't you give a good god damn? You're sorry?" His snort of derision left little to say. "That is the lie of the year!"

He leaped to his feet and strode over to her, his six feet two inches giving him now the stature of a colossus.

"One blessed word out of you to her and I make you this promise. You'll want to pull your tongue out by the roots when I'm through with you!" Leaving her shocked and shaken, he strode out to his car and drove off in a billowing cloud of yellow dust.

After a fruitless evening of searching, Jeff came wearily home and dropped exhausted and dispirited into a chair on the verandah. His daughter was in trouble. She had tried to kill herself, and her father, miserable and stricken, could do nothing.... The pipestem snapped between his teeth. He took it out of his mouth and stared at the jagged ends.

CHAPTER TWO

D R. ALCIDE FONTENOT SMOOTHED his black spade beard with long sensitive fingers and swallowed a sudden spurt of saliva initiated by a gust of air that had previously flowed over Maud's roast as she took it from the oven for basting. Maud could do wonderful things to a roast. He faced the man seated across the office from him and nodded vigorously. "Yes, I treated her because I had no choice in the matter. God knows how she managed it, but it is certain that some sharp instrument had been employed either by her or some clumsy abortionist. It was providential that she or they didn't go through the vaginal wall and into the peritoneal space. Death, then, would have been almost certain unless she had received immediate attention."

Jefferson Salton squirmed a little in his chair and gripped the bit of his pipe with a bulldog hold. His lean powerful jaw, strutted with hard muscle, showed a quivering nerve near the corner of his mouth. He ran his hand over his iron gray hair and tried to relax by slumping in his chair.

Dr. Fontenot eyed him keenly. "She's all right now, isn't she?"

"Perfectly," said Salton, removing his pipe and massaging the St. Vitic nerve. "In body, that is. It's her mind I fear for. I tried to get her to tell me who it was but she began to show signs of hysteria so naturally I let the matter drop. I was hoping that maybe she had told you."

The doctor shook his head. "Not a word did she tell me. Maybe I'd better tell you the whole thing as I know it."

"Yes, I'd like to know."

Dr. Fontenot, semi-retired physician, whistled merrily as he gave the finishing touches to a dry fly. Bits of hair and feathers littered the carpet and a bottle of metaphen stood nearby attesting, as did spots of the antiseptic adorning his fingers, to the doctor's not infrequent slips with both hook and knife.

Cars did not interest him overmuch as they passed on the street, but when he heard the crash of his fence and saw the coupe charging across Maud's roses, to come to a grinding sudden stop against his concrete steps, he was both pained and angry. He leaped to his feet and strode out on the porch. His furious speech died on his lips when he looked at the girl's face. It was deathly white and as he looked, she collapsed over the steering wheel, sending the horn into a fury of noise. As Maud came placidly out on the porch, he leaped youthfully to the ground and opened the door of the car.

He gasped, *"Sacré nom du petit cochon."* He called to Maud, "Come help me, Maud. The child is bleeding to death!"

They pulled her from the car and a great pool of blood was clotted on the leather of the seat. Her dress was soaked from waist to hem. Together they carried her into the doctor's office and minor surgery.

"She ought to go to the hospital," said Maud coolly. "I'll call the ambulance."

"You will do no such thing," said the little man rapidly. "There's something queer here." He raised the girl's dress and stripped off her blood-soaked panties. "See—what did I tell you. This is Jeff Salton's daughter and I'm sure he won't want this bruited about. Call Jane and tell her to locate Albert if she can and have him come home immediately. Now, if you'll get my instruments from the autoclave there—they've been run, haven't they?"

She nodded, "Yes, I ran them this morning."

"Good, I'll try to locate this bleeder and—Oh, yes, I'll want some triple zero silk suture and a small needle. For goodness sake, throw those little needle forceps away and get mine!"

"Albert likes the little ones," said Maud, placidly.

"Albert is a fool," he retorted testily, scrubbing his hands hard. After the prescribed seven minutes, he dried them on a sterile towel.

Maud opened a pair of sterile gloves and powdered his hands heavily.

"I'll manage now," he said. "Go see if you can locate Albert. No, put Jane on it and come on back. I may need help."

Antoinette Salton lay quiet and still in a deep drugged sleep and Dr. Fontenot watched her with bright black eyes. Her hair lay spread on the pillow like a shimmering blond veil and he could see the faint veins in her smooth lids. Her face was too strong to be pretty and her full firm jaw with its deeply cleft Salton chin dissipated the suggestion of weakness displayed by her full, somewhat petulant lips. The forehead was broad and high and the ridges of the brow were almost prominent. A decidedly striking face but more for its strength than its beauty. The little man moved the tiny goatee on his nether lip up and down in perplexity and vexation.

Albert, his son, came quietly in. "Mom says you did a good job on her."

"I always do a good job!" snapped his father. "You needn't talk so blasted low. She had morphine and luminal. Thunder wouldn't wake her. She'll be all right unless Jane's blood kills her."

"Did you get anything from her about...?"

"Not a word. She was in no condition to talk. It has me worried though. I'll have to tell Jeff about it because he'll be looking for her."

"He's a right guy," said Albert. "If it was ninety nine out of a hundred fathers, make something up I'd say, but not to him."

"Yes, that's true but … well, dammit! I like Jeff and … but he's got to be told so I'd better phone him." Dr. Fontenot left the room with a brisk stride and Albert looked at her for a while, frowning.

Dr. Fontenot sipped at his highball. "Well Jeff, there you are. That's all I know. During the week I had her here. I tried every way I could to get something out of her without actually pinning her down. I even tried that once and all I got was a shake of the head."

Salton gripped the arms of his chair and his teeth gritted on his pipestem. "Give me that bottle, Alcide," he ground out. Fontenot shrugged lightly and handed him the bottle. Salton placed it to his mouth and lowered the contents noticeably. He wiped his mouth delicately with a white handkerchief and handed the bottle back.

"Will that help?" asked the doctor.

Salton shrugged and renewed his grip on the dead pipe. "Answer your own question, you're the doctor."

"How much do you drink, Jeff?"

"Possibly a quart a day … a little more some days."

"And yet I've never seen you drunk."

Jeff smiled, showing his strong white teeth. "I've never been drunk in that sense and I've never had a hangover. I guess it'll kill me some day."

"I doubt," said the doctor, "that whiskey ever killed anyone *per se*. Hopeless dipsomaniacs often let their diet go to pot, or the same condition which caused the drinking likely produced a freshet of ulcers. By the way, Jeff, you're an intelligent man. What do you think makes you drink?"

Jeff spread his long-fingered hands out on the chair arms and considered them for a while before he spoke. "No single thing, Alcide. Dozens—hundreds—of things all gathered about my head and started buzzing. I can only still them with the bottle. My first mistake was marrying the second time or maybe it was the first time. I don't know. I do know that after a wife like Antoinette, I was a fool to expect the same stroke of fate which sent her to me to repeat. There never was a woman like her for me, at any rate, and she spoiled me utterly. When I married Lavender, a stupid name for a thistle, I apparently suffered from a complete mental blackout. Never, in all my drinking life, have I ever displayed so dull a wit."

"What," asked the doctor, puffing a flame into the end of a thin cheroot, "exactly is the matter with Lavender other than her appallingly stupid sense of values?"

"She is like many another, Alcide. Her stupidity might begin there, but that doesn't end it. She lives in the questionable sunlight of past ancestry. Some peasant grandfather who allegedly came over on the *Mayflower,* some malcontent or criminal or other miserable expatriate possibly has now been elevated to the stature of Charlemagne's brother-in-law or some such preposterous thing. As if that made any difference. A little reading in anthropology or genetics would dissipate all this ancestor worship."

Fontenot shook his head. "I doubt it. You are going on the assumption that they would be amenable to reason, which they are not. Wiggam pointed out that a few healthy near relatives are a lot more important than any number of interred and consequently sainted ancestors."

"Well you have made my point for me though I digressed in speculation. There is nothing in the world that will change such people's attitudes and Lavender, the thistle, has more than her share."

"Snobbery," put in Dr. Fontenot, "is probably one of the most drastic self-indictments ever seen. I say self-indictment because that is actually what it is. Not intentional, naturally, but true, none the less. It is one of the more pitiable methods of self-inflation detectable a mile off, and worse by far than streptococcus which, if left to its own devices kills with relative dispatch; whereas snobbery is slow death and invisible to all but a few of those very rare people who at long last make some serious effort at self-evaluation."

"Alcide, I curse myself that I haven't talked to you more in the past. You are an intellectual tonic."

"That is a high compliment, Jeff. I'll try to deserve it." The tone was ordinary but had a certain steely quality that jerked Salton away from an inspection of the whiskey bottle.

"You meant something then which you didn't put into words?"

The doctor poured out a generous portion of whiskey and added Coca Cola and ice. He faced Salton with characteristic suddenness. "Yes! I know I'm beginning to sound like Missy Blumendahl but I doubt that I could find a better one to emulate. She always dove headlong into a problem and vowed to solve it without having the remotest idea as to how she would accomplish it, but she always did. There are ways out of everything, Jeff, because problems are posed by the human brain. *Ergo,* no miracle will solve them, only the human mind can."

Jeff bit down on the stem of his pipe. "Before you put me down as schizoid, I'll admit that with a little more strength I might be able to do more. Drink is the milk of the weak and the aged. I'm not yet in the latter category so I come under the former. In other words, my problem as you have pointed out is my own fault in the essence. For instance, if I had had enough sense to steer clear of Lavender in the first place, I wouldn't have a problem to my name, unless I slipped up in some other fashion."

"Prescience," said Dr. Fontenot, "has been denied us. One has to accept the responsibility of his actions without being technically responsible for their birth."

"Then you don't believe in free will?"

The little man uttered an oath. "Man is an animal, Jeff, and a good half of his troubles would evaporate if he'd embrace the full array of implications and truths that fact projects. Free will, like everything else that the finite mind of man can grasp, has its limitations. You are free to. choose between cold and hot, soft and hard, sweet and bitter, practically anything that has to do with animal reaction and creature comfort but when you go against the animal self, then it is when the individual capacity comes to the fore. We do, under the pressure of social codes, about what we can and from there on in, it is a matter of avoiding discovery, avoiding punishment and scorn and justifying to ourselves such off-the-path exploration. The church rests its entire case on the absoluteness of free will because even in his somewhat childish mind a God who punished man for what he could not help would be a tyrant, indeed, therefore he is saddled with it from sheer necessity. Science and evidence, no matter how conclusive because in such a hierachy the edifice must endure no matter what the cost of the flock, will ever make an impression, I'm afraid."

Salton sighed and brutalized his pipe stem. "Living in Louisiana has I suppose taken a lot of the original whalebone from the Salton line. Here we live and let live. We are somewhat slothful and addicted to easy living. Some would call it degenerative processes at work."

"Speaking of that I'm reminded of that poor girl, Feathers Maidstone, sprung from a long line of eccentric aristocrats with money."

Jeff grimaced. "I need no reminding of that. As neighbors they are in my hair more than I would like to admit. Aristocrats who are so totally blind that Old Obadiah Maidstone and Jessica pretend to be in flat ignorance of their daughter's gluttonous sex cravings. Every Negro on the plantation flees into hiding the first glimpse he gets of her. It is a wonder she hasn't caused some poor Negro to be lynched. I can imagine the ire of the countryside should such a thing get about in the right circles. It is sad and distressing."

The doctor nodded. "I think that her utter lack of pretense is her only virtue. She is quite open except in company and I've seen her absolutely tortured by some circumstance that kept her on good behavior for a space—say some social function of sorts."

"Yes," said Jeff, whimsically. "Like one of Lavender's teas. I'm tortured by them too because they sometimes cut me off from my room or office and I either have to barge through and get tripped into a lot of stupid guff or I stay and wait till they've had their fill of deploring the generally poor breeding of the world as a whole and guessing whose wife has managed to perform a perfect assignation."

"It has been talked about," said the doctor, tossing his cheroot away, "that poor Feathers will submit to the attentions of anyone if she is tortured too much."

"Entirely possible," said Jeff. "I recall once she caught me down by Big Buff Creek. To say she was mad would be mild. I had just taken a swim when she came tearing up on that big red horse. She had evidently seen me and made preparations. Before I knew it she had practically assaulted me right there on the creek bank."

"Did she?"

Jeff smiled ruefully. "Well, I can tell you it was an experience I'm not likely to forget soon."

"I'm sure you won't," agreed the doctor. "Only a medical man who has had a number of women on his list of patients could thoroughly sympathize with you."

Jeff mauled his pipe ruminatively. "I guess you could say that a great deal of my present condition is because of a certain moral cowardice, the shrinking away from unpleasantness and the eternal hope that somehow things would work themselves out."

The doctor shook his head. "As to that I refuse to go on record. What I should like is the omniscience necessary to envision you as a savage on a tiny Pacific isle without a single spot of civilized taint. It is a mortal impossibility to say what is heredity and what is environment as regards the whimsies of human conduct."

Jeff nodded in agreement. "My father and I are good examples of that. Same environment and close blood ties and yet his principal morality seemed that of observing good taste. I am, on the other hand, beset by all sort of fears of social indictment. That is certainly not like him."

"Recalling your father with some clarity, I should say it is a pity," commented Fontenot dryly.

"Granny Rosa intimated the same thing the other night. In fact, in a few words, she told me a number of things I hadn't known, or admitted, which is much the same thing."

Dr. Fontenot built himself a highball and handed the bottle to Jefferson.

Jeff shook his head. "I think I'll let it slide for a while. That's what talking to you does for me."

The doctor tasted his drink and lighted a cheroot. "Now, Jeff, allow me to point out the ramifications of that single difference between you and your father—but first let me ask you a few questions. What was your sex life before marriage?"

Jeff flushed. "If anyone else had asked me that…."

"No one else did," snapped the old man, "answer the question!"

"Well, as I recall, there was a great deal of experimentation and clumsy fumbling which stood me in poor stead when I finally married."

The other nodded with satisfaction. "A normal thing, in spite of those who are convinced that at the age of twenty one they are suave artistic wolves. Now, what about your marriage to Antoinette?"

There was a sad but delighted gleam in Jeff's eyes. "Like nothing ever seen in this world," he breathed, looking backward through the happy years. "At tea, at dinner, at a dance, Antoinette was as fine a lady as ever walked but in the bedroom she was the most accomplished savage that mind can imagine. I'll never forget how she took my breath away. The only thing that kept her activities from shocking me was her absolute genius in lighting the fire in me. Never once during our entire life together did sex acquire the routine habitualness that I'm sure happens often. Never once did she invade a contrary mood, or place me in the position of performing to please her."

The doctor sighed. "One of the more stellar accomplishments of the clever woman who suffers, doubtlessly, from the lack of equal cleverness in the male. Now, tell me what your sex life has been with Lavender?"

Jeff shuddered. "That is one I was hoping you would miss. In short, it has been nothing. She was frightened half out of her mind at first, then when after the expenditure of much careful effort I quelled her fears, she was about as attractive in bed as a corpse. She freely admitted that the whole idea revolted her and made it plain that since it was her duty she would suffer bravely."

Dr. Fontenot grimaced. "Such women should be spayed at birth if there was some way to detect them. Then they'd grow hair on their faces and at least be detectable. But that's another matter. Last question, how long have you and she had separate rooms?"

Again Jeff flushed. "Three years ago, after a particularly repugnant scene I suggested it. It had gotten to the point that had she lighted a cigarette or read a book during the act, it would have been no less obvious that the whole proceeding was a rattling bore."

"And since that time?"

Jeff took fresh purchase on his pipe and picked up the whiskey bottle. "Nothing … no one. This drink I'm about to take, in no way reflects on the turn of your conversation. It is merely," he shook the bottle, "the introduction to my mistress. She never fails me." He drank deeply. "Nor does she ever come up wanting. She performs too well if anything."

"And that," said the doctor sharply, "is the exact point of my questions. You drank like any gay blade before marriage. Married to Antoinette, you probably drank socially. Since Lavender has been on the scene you have been pouring it down. I ask you what would your father have done under like circumstances?"

Jeff tamped rough tobacco in his pipe and lighted it. "First off, he wouldn't have had Lavender on a horse trade. If he had, just on a supposition, he'd have left her to her ways and taken on some sharp female to provide what she couldn't."

Dr. Fontenot sighed. "Well, there you are. He lived for himself and with other people. You're living for other people and raising hell with yourself. Society would, of course, have another set of terms for that and go their merry way doing as they wished and hiding it. The difference there is that they haven't the guts to dredge up a bit of fundamental honesty. That's why the matter drives so many of them bats. One has to get along, I'll admit that, but it need not creep into one's conversation with one's self and so distort things that it become a virtual impossibility to have any self-honesty, the lack of which mental deterioration is made of."

Jeff rose to his feet. "Alcide, I want you to promise to let me come again. I'll have to be getting along now because I don't want to work Granny Rosa to death. She hasn't hardly left the room since Toni came home. I certainly don't want Lavender to find her alone and have a chance to get in some of her kind of sympathy."

"By all means, Jeff," said the little man bounding to his feet, "and some day when I haven't anything to do, I'll visit you and we'll blot up a few highballs. I'll want to see Toni in a couple of days anyhow."

Jeff grasped the older man by the hand. "You've made me feel better than I have in years. You have done my daughter and me a great favor and I assure you that neither of us will forget it."

Fontenot wriggled. "I do what I can for my fellow man, Jeff. I have no religion of the usual sort but I love my fellow man for all his faults and I hold out a hand whenever I can."

CHAPTER THREE

ONI LAY VERY STILL ON HER BACK and stared at the ceiling. The sheets were clean and cool, smelling of the ancient wooden drawers where they had been stored. Granny Rosa sat nearby and nodded in her chair, having found that her Sugar Doll either had nothing to say or was not in the mood for conversation. A discreet knock sounded on the door.

Granny awoke with a start, "Who dat?"

"It's me, Granny," came Jeff's voice. "Is Toni asleep?"

"Nawssuh, you can come in."

Jeff opened the door and walked swiftly to the bed. "Feel all right, Kitten?"

Toni managed a smile and nodded. "I feel sort of dead, Pop, that's all."

"I saw Dr. Fontenot today. He says you'll be all right."

"Yes sir."

Jeff felt helpless. Toni agreed with no enthusiasm whatever, and things had been like this for days. He turned to Granny Rosa. "You can go, Granny. I'll stay with her now."

Granny stood up. "I could manage with some res' myself. I ain't ever got Monday's ironin' done yet, neither."

"Why don't you make Odele help you?"

"Cause Odele ain't got nuff sense to feed herself, let alone momuckin' up my linens."

After the old woman had gone, Jeff took a chair and lighted his pipe. "I'm your father, Kitten," he began, "but I guess somewhere I've failed you."

She shook her head slowly. "No, Pop."

"Yet when you got in trouble, I was the last to know about it. I should have moulded things so that I would have been the first."

"It's not that simple."

"Then let's talk about it. You're not in the right frame of mind and you know it."

"What sort of mind should a person have that has done what I have?" Her pale face was set and her mouth a white slash in her face.

Jeff gnawed savagely at his pipe stem. "Doesn't the fact that you had nothing to do with what happened make any difference?"

"The thing which has me flat on my back and sick to death of me, hating me for a murderer is of my own doing." Her voice tottered and almost fell into a break.

The muscles across his shoulders grew so taut they ached. He clasped his hands tightly and tried to keep his mind from knotting up into flickers of confused thought.

It wasn't the whiskey today, he told himself, because he hadn't had that much. He turned tired eyes on her. "Kitten, I want to help you. Dr. Fontenot wants to help you and Granny wants to help you. None of us can if you won't let us. You'll have to help."

She turned her face away and remained silent. For a long time there was silence, then she faced him again. "Pop, will you come sit by me?"

He sat on the edge of the bed and held her hands.

"Pop, you know I love you, don't you?"

His voice was husky. "Yes, Kitten, I know you do."

Tears came to her eyes. "Something terrible has happened, Pop. I can't control it ... I just know something's gone. That awful night—that terrible old woman, her instruments—the pain ..." She broke into uncontrollable weeping and Jeff lifted her against his chest and held her close while she cried herself out, then he laid her back against the pillow and sang to her in a rich low baritone. He sang her an old lullaby at which she smiled tenderly at first, then her face relaxed comfortably and she slept. He watched her for some time, then tiptoed from the room.

He sat by the old crank phone in the dim cool hall and asked to be connected with Dr. Alcide Fontenot in Kenton. The sleepy Port Hull operator yawned and said, "Thangkew."

"Alcide, this is Jeff. It pains me to call you this soon even though you said you wanted to help with. ..." A burst of angry French at the other end of the line made him smile.

"All right, all right! Talk English, won't you? From here you sound like a flock of blackbirds gabbling."

"Never mind your blasted Anglo-Saxon insults," the little man shot back. "What's the trouble?"

"It's Toni. She is overcome by the enormity of her act and I can't get to her. She has erected a wall of resistance that I can't get through. I can't make her talk."

"Well, goddammit, let the girl alone!" snapped the doctor. "She isn't well yet and has your youth been so long ago that you have entirely forgotten that everything seemed twice as bad then as when you grew up?"

Jeff bowed his head. "I wish you'd come to see her," he begged humbly. "I'm afraid she'll try to do away with herself."

"I doubt that, but I'll come if it will make you feel any better."

"Please do. You have no idea how much better it will make me feel."

"I warn you, Jeff, I'll look at her but unless she's a lot better, I'm not going to try to talk to her."

"That, of course, is up to you but please come. Try to make it for supper."

Lemuel Patterstall slouched across the front yard toward the house. He had been drinking as usual and as usual he had a noticeable list.

Jeff's snort of disgust reached the ears of Lavender who sat on the porch twenty feet away. She looked around. "You say one word to my brother and I'll ...."

"You'll do what?" he snarled.

She sat back with a hurt look on her face. As a face it was singularly unattractive this afternoon. It had been too hot for her nap and Lavender was one of those people whose routine must go through unbroken or it upset her whole day. Her hair was done up behind her head in an unattractive knot accentuating the poverty of her facial structure and slightly receding chin.

Jeff shuddered and looked at Lemuel as he came up the steps. He was rather large but his shoulders were narrow and his hips wide. He had a peculiar sour-bitter smell that hung about him at all times like cheap perfume. His face was the counterpart of his sister's and his gross body gave the eerie impression that it had once belonged to someone else. His eyes were piggy and furtive and as far as Jeff knew, he had never shed a drop of honest sweat. As he reached the top step, his feet became intangled with each other, causing him to fall heavily and roll in a wild flurry of arms and legs to the bottom of the steps.

Jeff fell back in his chair and roared with mirth, not noticing the look of murderous hatred cast in his direction by his brother-in-law. Lavender leaped to her feet. "Come into the office, Jefferson. I want to talk to you."

Inside the office, she said, "Are you deliberately trying to get rid of us?"

Jeff looked her over coolly. "It wouldn't be a half bad idea."

"It can be accomplished," she retorted furiously, "for a price. Just one more scene like that last one and you'll find out what the price is."

"If I had had a higher set of steps, I think half the problem would have solved itself," said Jeff grinning furiously. "Why don't both of you fall off the roof and break your necks?"

She stared at him a long time. "Neither of us will be that easy to get rid of. Have no illusions about that, Jeff, dear."

"Any illusions I had about you and Lem, and there must have been a power of them at one time, have long since gone by the board. If I had the guts of a fly I'd kick both of you off Fomalhaut and be rid of you."

"But you won't do that, will you, dear? If you did, it might get circulated about that your daughter was raped and had an abortion performed."

Jeff's long fingers drove nails into the palms of his hands like spikes into soft wood. Stark murder gleamed in his usually mild eyes. "I doubt, Lavvy," he said, using a nickname which she loathed, "that you'll ever *fall* from anything!" He stopped to readjust his breathing which was threatening to drive the blood through his skin. "But it would be just as effective to *throw you off the top of the house!*" He leaned forward and delivered the last words with such vitriolic malignance that she recoiled a couple of paces. Breath whistled through his distended nostrils and he took a step toward her. "Think that over, my dear. Just let me get the barest suggestion of any such thing and that'll be the day you putrid, crawling, yellow bitch snake!"

Jeff stalked from the office and back to his seat on the porch. He was weak and trembling and needed a drink but refused to take one.

Lemuel walked up and down in his sister's room massaging his damp hands. "You should be more careful, learn to control yourself. Suppose he would run us off? What would we do then? I doubt that you'd interest the chorus boys any more."

She strode forward and slapped him with all her strength. "Say that again and I'll kill you."

He sat down rubbing his face with a curious avidity, and seemed neither hurt nor angry. She watched him for a moment and her face underwent a subtle change. Quickly she closed the blinds, effectively darkening the room, went to a closet and came back with a short many-tailed whip. There was a short whispered conversation, a rustling sound, then the swishing crack of the whip, groans, and from the woman's mouth a stream of obscenities, vicious, revolting, and delivered with a weird crooning gusto.

"Well, as I told you over the phone, Jeff, she's not ready for your blundering psychotherapy, yet."

Jeff nodded numbly. "You're right, I suppose, but this thing is killing me. I'm afraid for her mind."

"Oh, pish!" scoffed the doctor. "Her mind's probably a lot more stable than yours. However, I'll see what I can do."

As they walked down the big upstairs hall to Toni's room Fontenot stopped him. "I'll go the rest of the way, alone, thank you. I don't want any fathers in my way when I talk to my patients."

Jeff nodded and stopped. He watched the doctor open the door and close it, then he turned slowly and walked down the long winding stairway through the downstairs hall, on to the broad verandah here he slumped into a chair.

Dr. Fontenot breezed into the room. "Well, how's my patient this evening?"

She looked at him but didn't speak immediately. When she did, her voice was small and disembodied. "I want to thank you, Doctor, for what you did. I'm really very grateful."

He frowned. "Nonsense. Right in my own front yard—front steps to be exact. What else could I do?"

She smiled slightly as he sat on the bed. "Be self-effacing, then."

"I'm tickled pink that I could help, my dear. Self-effacement is a gesture. I'm really flattered." He pulled the covers down and palpated her abdomen. "Any pain, there?"

"No sir. It's still a little sore but it doesn't hurt." He nodded and felt gently of a firm breast. She gasped a little and flinched.

"How long, my dear ... how long was it ... ?"

"Six weeks, I think—thereabouts."

"Ummm, hummm, too soon for any noticeable lactation."
He pulled the covers up again and let his glance wander over her.

"You seem to be in good shape now, physically. Why are you
trying to freeze your father out?"

Tears sprang into her eyes. "I'm awful, I'm a murderer."

His breath hissed in sharply. "Every woman is a murderer
and every man also every time birth control is used successfully."

"Oh, no ...."

"And pray why not?" He placed a gentle hand over hers as it
lay flaccid on the coverlet. "You see, Toni, such things are unfortunate and wholly undesirable, but just the same they happen.
I brought up an extreme, but it contains some element of truth
as certain sects have long maintained for reasons of their own. I
mentioned an extreme to show you that you are trying to be an
extremist. The only difference is one of degree.

"In your case you were driven to your deed by the consciousness of what society would think, knowing that as long
as they are kept in the dark you may enjoy all the privileges of
and be called the nicest of girls, no matter what you do out of
their sight."

Dr. Fontenot continued talking to her in his soft kind voice
drawing out her opinions, exposing them and attacking them
with furious barrages of crystal logic.

She listened fascinated, uplifted, and at times frightened. "I
don't think I ever heard things explained quite like that before,"
she said at length.

"A great pity," he shot back. "Had you been reared to know
these things you would have taken your trouble in stride and it
wouldn't have thrown you like this and you would have managed
things better. Had I not been on the scene, luckily, you might
now be dead. Be thankful that you're not."

"The way you put it, it makes sense but ...."

"I know. You were given the facts as viewed from a rational angle. If you cannot fit them into your own mind, it is certain that no one can do it for you. What I'm concerned about is what effect it has had on you in your man-woman relationship."

She turned her head away from him and for a long time did not speak. When she did there was hatred in her voice. "I never want another man to touch me as long as I live. I think I'd kill him if he touched me like that." She rose to a sitting position, her eyes blazing and her face white and twitching. A hard convulsive shudder shook her and she bit her lips to keep back a cry. Dr. Fontenot put his face close to hers.

"*Stop that!*" His voice had the hard explosive command of a gun shot. It frightened her a little and she breathed better. "Now lie back and relax." It was a soothing order which he accompanied with firm hands on her shoulders that shoved her back to the pillow.

"Now, young woman, I forbid you to think about this thing any more for the present. Get out of that bed and recover physically. Then I promise to beat you to death with that unnatural attitude." If he had hoped to win a smile from her, he was disappointed. She only retreated deeper into the cover, her eyes still taut with anguish and revulsion.

Dr. Fontenot found Salton on the porch sunk deep in reverie. "Have a chair, Alcide, and what about a highball?"

"Never ask me that," said the little man. "Just bring it along and I'd advise you to have a long snort, yourself."

"You would?"

"I would, indeed. You've been off it ever since Toni's trouble and it's tying you in knots. Save that will power for some worthy cause or, better still, to temper your quantity."

Jeff raised his voice, "Odele?"

A tall colored girl came gracefully along the porch from the west side of the house.

"Did you call, sir?"

Jeff stared. "Where's Odele? Who're you?"

"I'm Granny Rosa's granddaughter, sir. Odele is ... going to have a family. I took her place."

"You're Archie's daughter?"

"Yes, sir."

"When did you arrive?"

"A week ago, sir. Father died not long ago, you know?"

Jeff nodded. "Yes, I was sorry to hear that, but I.... Well, anyway, you seem capable and you speak well. Did you attend school?"

"Yes sir, I finished high school and went to business college."

"Hope you like it here," Jeff finished lamely, realizing that he had been conducting an inquiry. "Will you bring a bridge table, some Coca Cola, ice and a bottle of whiskey? There should be a bottle on the sideboard in the dining room."

She nodded respectfully. "Yes, sir."

Dr. Fontenot fixed a pair of bright blue eyes on Jeff, till the other began to feel hot and uncomfortable.

"Er hummm," began the doctor, "holding out on me, eh?"

"Really, Alcide, that's the first time I ever saw her."

"Likely story," scoffed the doctor. "But no matter, I don't know who Archie is but I will say that he did well by the girl. Her skin is amber, gold and honey, and my God! What a figure! Generosity certainly missing in no place."

Jeff became acutely uncomfortable. The sight of the girl had shaken him sorely and wakened things he had thought dead. He tried to be casual. "Oh, sure ..." and failed.

The other cackled delightedly. "Just what you need, and don't try to get cagy with me. I've seen more than any hundred men and have experienced more than any ten you can name. I think she's beautiful, don't you?"

Jeff suffered, but nodded. "Yes, I guess she is at that, but ...."

Fontenot snorted. "But what? Just because she has colored blood in her? Phooey! I thought you were a man of the world.

Trouble with you good old Anglo-Saxons is that you still have that lodge meeting attitude about everything. Any fool could see that she shook you where you live, and yet you want to pretend it is nothing really. Thank God I'm a Frenchman with the ability to get outside myself. I'd burst if I didn't."

Jeff tossed down half a gill and cleared his throat. "What about Toni?"

The old man put his highball down carefully and lighted a cheroot before answering. "I don't like it."

Jeff didn't have to question that statement and for a while they were silent, gazing past the mighty shadowy columns onto the moon splashed lawn. The night was a good deal cooler than the day had been and the atmosphere had some motion. Miles away, a tugboat towing a long string of barges swept the sky with the misty finger of a searchlight. The mournful hoot-hoot of its whistle came to them faintly.

Jeff loaded his pipe and lit it. "What, exactly, don't you like?"

Dr. Fontenot sat his drink on the floor and sighed. "Principally her attitude toward sex. The shock and horror of that night will wear off but the first time some lad wants to do a little mild necking, she's going to bust him one in the puss and he's going to be mildly surprised to say the least."

"She *should* slap the hell out of him," said Jeff frowning. "I don't want my daughter...."

Dr. Fontenot smote the arm of the chair vehemently. "Jefferson, you may poison me with your liquor or shoot me with your gun but pray do not bore me."

Jeff grinned weakly, "Okay, I take it all back."

Fontenot sniffed. "Do, for heaven's sake, then go bury it far away."

"I guess it's just hard to grow out of."

"Probably, but just remember that to ever grow into it, you had to bruise every natural impulse you ever had. How old were you, Jeff, when you had your first necking session?"

Jeff flushed, grateful for the dark. "Twenty. I had pecked about before then, but the first real one was twenty. I'm afraid both of us got sort of carried away in the rush...."

"Naturally, naturally. You were lucky that her father didn't come searching for you with a shotgun."

Jeff leaned back and savaged the stem of his pipe. "I seem to recall wondering afterward why anything so wonderful could be wrong. I was too young to see what the dangers were."

"Many a similar wonder has wended its way heavenward," said the doctor.

"And you think Toni is going to have trouble along those lines?"

The other nodded. "She is, and it is a national pity, a horrible waste of good woman flesh, the like of which is seldom found. The thought of her being ruined like that makes me ill. You still have no idea who it could have been?"

"Not the slightest. The storm had Lavender and me both stranded. She at the MacAllisters' and I in Port Hilton. She was alone, except for..." Jeff came upright in his chair, his eyes gleaming hellishly. "Lemuel was here," he ground out, breathing heavily.

Fontenot waved his hands madly. "Let's not go rushing to conclusions and acting foolishly. Remember, it was pitch dark. So far, we haven't a word from her. If she knows, she isn't talking and any move made now would be without information, therefore, foolish. Right now, there is nothing to do but to wait. Time has a way of taking care of such things." He finished his drink and got up. "Have to go now, Jeff. Maud will be wondering whether I've had a wreck. Just stick tight and let the girl alone. In fact, I forbid that you even hint at the subject."

Dr. Fontenot turned out his lights before he reached the cabin and with a deft twitch of the wheel, tooled the drab little coupe off the road and stopped beneath a big spreading china tree. It was in full bloom and its flowers had draped a cloak of heavy perfume over the immediate area. He stepped from the car and undid the chain latch on the picket gate. A cur set up a terrific clamor effectively halting the doctor till a bellow from the house drove the dog scampering under the house to peer out with suspicion but silent. Granny Rosa's discipline was as effective with animals as with people. She waddled to the door and stood silhouetted by the weak rays of the oil lamp. "Who dat?"

"Call off your dogs, Granny. It's Dr. Fontenot."

"Do Jesus," she bellowed. "Come in, doctuh, come on in. I ain't seen you since de time us tuck dat 'flicted thaing from Josie Tillis wid a plow line."

"Quiet," said the doctor as he mounted the porch, grinning. "Don't advertise our methods. People might talk."

"Let 'em talk. Dey does ennyhow. Set down and... Coppercawn! Git some o' dat jewberry wine outa de loft and pour de doctuh a glassful. Hit's three years old, doctuh, and strong as a deck o' fawties."

"Coppercorn?"

"Yassuh, dat's Archie's chile. Archie was mah fus' boy. Died last month wid de high blood and hart trubbel."

A little tingle went over the doctor. He'd welcome a chance to see the girl under a better light. His first impression had been distinctly delightful.

She came out presently and he could tell she wore only a single cotton garment. The effect was nothing short of electric. Her long powerful legs showed plainly through the thin garment, her breasts seemed about to burst through the straining cloth and her waist was slim and long. "Dis Dr. Fontenot, Coppercawn," said Granny proudly.

The little man rose and took her strong shapely hand. "How are you, Coppercorn. Sounds like one of Granny's names."

"How do you do, sir—yes, it is. I was named for the tropic."

"Oh—Capricorn!"

"Yes, sir." He accepted the drink and sat down.

"Fine looking girl, Granny. She's awfully light, though."

Granny laughed. "Sho she is. Might nigh white. Couldn't tell de difference on a night like dis here one. 'Tain't no wonder, though. Her mammy was a bright gal, too and ... well, you ought t' know. Me and you brung both of 'em." She motioned with her head and the girl obediently went back in the house.

"We did what?"

"Men you. Us d'livered both dem chillun ... oh, way back in sebenteen. Member, I sont fer you cause I knowed dey wuz twins and I wuz skeered I wasn't smaht nuff t' d'liver 'em by mahself?"

He smote his leg. "Well, I'll be damned. What do you know ...?" A crafty look came over his face. He glanced back in the house and seeing that Capricorn was not in hearing, he said in a low voice, "Remember what she told us that night before she died?"

Granny nodded soberly. "Sho do but dey don't know it. I ain't never told 'em."

"Did you ever tell Archie?"

"No suh, I ain't tole him neither. I don't see no sense telling sompn' whut ain't gonna do no good and kin do a lota' harm."

He nodded vigorously. "A sentiment that should be allowed to spread."

"A which?"

"Good idea, I mean. Let's see, some wise man put it this way. 'A truth that harms one without helping another loses its virtue.' No need for Archie to know that they were a white man's children."

"Yassuh," agreed Granny hazily. "I reckon so ...."

"Where's the other one ... she stay in New Orleans?"

"Nawsuh, you didn't see her at de house?"

He drank the rest of the wine and smacked his lips. "This has been a night of surprises, Granny. Twins, and I thought it was the same one. Then it turns out that you and I delivered them. I came by here to ask you something."

"Ax it," she said with a chuckle. "Gawd knows, I owes you a few favors. You done me plenty."

"When I saw that girl at the house I began to think. She said Odele was about to have a family. When I saw Odele two weeks ago, she couldn't have been over two months. Now what goes on here?"

Granny grinned mysteriously. "Oh—leetle idee o' mine. I handles things at de house. Dat Yankee woman ain't got nuff sense to po' water on a fiah and she don't care. De boss glad to have me 'round and so's mah Sugar Baby. So I 'ranged thaings t' suit mahself."

He flicked his beady eyes over the old woman's placid face. "That's what I'm getting at. Odele could have worked another three or four months."

"Not'n git her chile brung free she couldn't."

He grinned delightedly. "Now we're getting closer to pay dirt. *Why* did you want to replace Odele?"

Granny grinned widely. "I axt you once how you knowed sumpn' and you said, 'Granny, ah knows everything.' You figger hit out fo' youself."

CHAPTER FOUR

BULL FALLON WALKED ALONG THE woodsy path with a light and springy step in spite of his work-hardened two hundred pounds of bone and muscle. He had "breshed up" against Marthy Petersen at the supper and things had begun to happen. Marthy was lush and sultry and high brown and tonight she was being left severely alone, due to the razor wielding proclivities of her escort who was temporarily absent getting some pink lemonade for himself and his girl.

Marthy glanced at him coquettishly out of veiled eyes and whispered. "What's the matter, Bull, you 'fraid of a razor too?"

Bull stiffened. "*Who?*"

"*You!*"

Bull glanced about and saw Prince Jones buying two glasses of lemonade at the makeshift counter against the wall of Phillydelfy Washington's house.

"I ain't no trouble maker," he announced loftily, and leaned back against the house. Marthy turned her back to him and leaned back. The hot soft pressure of her buttocks sent blood leaping through his veins and his left hand crept around her waist.

"Oooowee," she moaned softly and pressed harder against him. They were somewhat protected by the insufficiency of the lights which were kerosene-filled wine bottles with old twists of quilts for wicks. Prince had to do a little searching before he found her and when he did, the sight did not amuse him.

He dropped the lemonade to the ground and said, "Come out hyer."

"She can't come," said Bull, whose previous resolution not to start trouble had departed.

"How come she can't come?"

"Cause I got her."

"Den you turn her loose."

"Go git lost, pal" said Bull, contemptuously, recalling a line he had heard in a mystery play on the boss's radio.

"One boy in de hospittle now, cause he played 'roun wid mah wimmen," pointed out Prince, his right hand sliding into his back pocket with a significance that was not lost to either Marthy or Bull. With a sweep of his hand Bull tossed her aside and as the razor came from Prince's pocket it continued on its way out of the circle of light as though he had thrown it. Bull's mighty hand had closed over the smaller man's wrist and flicked it with such irresistible power that the fingers lost their grip on the weapon. Then with a contemptuous twist, Bull broke the arm and hurled Prince into a moaning heap. The other Negroes looked on with interest.

"Hit don' pay to muck up wid dat Bull," said Uncle Rafe Lee, "razor or no razor."

"You sed whut Gawd love," agreed Uncle Alvin Mack, maneuvering lemonade deftly around the quid of Days Work which swelled one side of his cadaverous face. "Ole pappy of his'n wuz de same way."

"Sho wuz," piped Si Witherspoon, a weazened little dwarf of a man who had always wanted to be big and brash. "I mind de time he tuck'n bet de boss's daddy he could butt de head outen a po'k ba'l. He done it too."

Bull, after a glance at Prince, whirled and walked away from the house. A hundred feet down the path, Marthy caught up with him. "Bull, wait."

"Whut fer," he rasped. "You ain't good for nuthin' but stahtin' trouble. Go home."

As Bull walked along the path through the woods, he wondered if he'd reach John Harrel's old house before the rain came. He hoped so. He already had grass stains on his new blue slacks and the boss was sure to have to kid him about them. He wondered if he dared try to remove the stains with soap and water. The first drop plopped in the dust ahead of him with an audible sound and in the distance he could hear the drumming roar of the rain. He broke into an easy long striding run.

He leaped nimbly up on the crumbling porch as the first of the rain thundered on the dry, warped, shingled roof like hail. Lightning ripped a blinding burst of blue flame which might have showed him the big red horse tied to a fig tree in the yard but Bull wasn't looking for horses.

He flung the door open and closed it with a bang almost fainting from fright the next instant. In the flare of the bolt, he saw that the house was already occupied. His gin went out of him so suddenly that it left a strange empty buzzing in his head. Standing now between him and the door was Feathers Maidstone. The lightning was almost continuous now, showing her taut angular face, the hard ruggedness of her not unlovely body and the strained intentness of her green eyes. She was dressed in a polo shirt and blue jeans when he first saw her, and seconds later, it seemed she was a beautiful and terrifying vision.

Bull, his teeth chattering with terror, whirled with very intention of hurling himself bodily through the window but a rattling snarl stopped him. Between him and the only means of escape stood a great Belgian police dog, his fangs gleaming in the flickering light. Feathers caught Bull about the waist and with surprising strength threw his palsied body to the floor, half stunning him. He could feel her hands roving over him, her voice and her words babbling and hardly coherent. "Be good, Bull. Be good. I won't hurt you Bull, be good." He shivered and lay still because he was too frightened to do otherwise. She caught his hands and passed them around her body, panting hard. Bull sent a short prayer to his maker and gave up.

It was nearly dawn when Bull opened the door of his house. His sister was just getting up to cook breakfast and he smelled the strong odor of coffee parching in the little wood stove. He mounted the porch steps and staggered as he reached the top. He felt sick and feverish and he was so weak he could hardly stand.

"Whut the matter, Bull? Wheh you been all night?"

"Shet up," he said shortly, "and bring me some coffee."

She went back to the kitchen and brought him coffee. His hand jerked so that the cup chattered against his teeth before he could steady it with his lips.

"You sho looks terrible," offered Alice. "You looks sick."

"I done tole you t' shet up," he snarled. "Ain't nuthin' wrong wid me. Hit's Sunday and I'm gonna git me some sleep. I ain't had no sleep." He beamed inwardly at his facile excuse. "Dat whut wrong wid me. I ain't had no sleep."

Alice looked him over critically taking in his ruined and stained slacks.

"Dem pants needs more'n sleep," she averred, turning away from him and entering the kitchen. He looked at his slacks. She had spoken the truth. They would be good for nothing except field work from now on, even if he had the nerve to wear them to work which he doubted. The boss would have the laugh of his life if he could see those pants now...

Feathers rode her horse slowly toward the big old house. It was one of those relics of past days which were so plentiful in St. Joseph's Parish as well as St. Louis and other nearby parishes. The big horse stepped lightly through the water that rushed noisily in the ditches. Rain still fell in tiny misty drops cooling her hot face. She swayed dreamily in the saddle and throbbed with satiety, caressing her bruises with a tender hand. Never had she been so roughly used yet so completely satisfied but she knew it wouldn't be for long.

At the crumbling old barn she unsaddled the horse and turned him into a stable where she fed and rubbed him down. She leaned against his warm back leg and rubbed her body against it. The sting of his sweat burned a skinned place on her arm and she deliberately rubbed it on him, savoring the astringent bite of the salt. King, the great dog, whined and nuzzled her hand. She left the stable and led the dog to the hallway of the barn. She stroked his flank and he whined expectantly. At one end of the barn there was a room filled with cotton seed. She led him to the door, opened it, and he went in.

CHAPTER FIVE

Albert Fontenot sat with his father in the living room complaining bitterly because the backwoods women would only come in when they were having trouble with childbirth. "At least they could come in and get an occasional check. Now I might lose both mother and child out of this caesarean this morning."

Dr. Fontenot lighted a cheroot. "You have your troubles and I have mine."

"You mean at the Saltons'?"

"Yes. Trouble of the sort I'd like to see wiped out once and for all."

Albert grinned tiredly. "All right, wipe it out."

"Don't be any bigger fool than you have to. How would I go about that?"

Albert shrugged. "I'm sure I don't know. I'll bet she now has a full blown revulsion toward anything sexual since that bad time she had!"

Jane came into the living room and handed the older Fontenot a highball. "You want one?" she asked Albert.

"No ... can't. Have an operation at one o'clock."

"Yes," barked his father suddenly.

"Yes what?"

"You're right. She is revolted at the mere idea of a man."

"Well since you're the happiness doctor why don't you vaccinate her?"

The little man's beard danced angrily. "Albert, I'm tempted to beat you over the head with a blunt instrument. Happiness, that is to say the contentment most people think of, is nothing but sloth and in sloth there can be no progress. Suppose Columbus had been satisfied to sit in Genoa and drink wine? Suppose men like Charcot had been happy, contented, and non-productive? In contemporary times suppose men like Fermi, Bush, Einstein, Oppenheimer and others had been content to make deodorants, tooth paste, and fruit salts?"

"We wouldn't have had the atom bomb," said Albert triumphantly.

"Right," shot back his father, "and Germany would. Where would we be now?"

"I give up," said Albert grinning.

The older doctor was pulling his beard victoriously when Maud came into the living room. "Missy Blumendahl is on the phone."

Dr. Fontenot frowned. "Now what does she want?"

Missy Blumendahl was St. Louis Parish's undisputed social empress. She gave parties at which practically everyone could be found basking in her reflected light. She was rich and eccentric, admitting privately that her parties were conceived that she might laugh at the antics of those who came.

"Hello," she bellowed over the phone. "That you, Alcide?"

"Yes, Missy, what's the trouble?"

"A pain in the gut, and, by God, I want you out here on the double!"

"I've retired," he told her shortly. "I'll send Albert out."

"Albert can't come," she retorted. "He has a caesarean this evening. Anyhow, I don't want any young jackanapes jogging me in the belly."

"The last time you had a pain in the gut," he reminded her, "I found you eating onion and sardine sandwiches, chasing them with beer."

"Look, you clabberheaded superannuated rake! I said I have a pain in the gut and I do. Get out here or you'll have a corpse on your hands." She hung up with a crash.

When Dr. Fontenot arrived at Fahenstock, Missy's ancestral pile of brick, columns, and pink plaster, the mistress was reclining in her bedroom clad in innumerable yards of lavender chiffon, emitting a smell which suggested Bradsher's Special Age Bourbon.

She rose to her feet, noticeably favoring her right leg. "Come in," she brayed loudly. "Sit down."

Dr. Fontenot felt driven bodily into his chair.

She made a face. "Pain in my right side, Alcide. I believe I have appendicitis."

He rose and gestured toward the bed. "Spill yourself on the bed."

She did so and the big four-poster creaked alarmingly because Missy weighed in the neighborhood of two hundred pounds. She laid her head carefully on the pillow so as not to disturb her tightly waved yellow hair.

"Ow…dammit!" As the doctor touched a sore spot. "That's where it hurts."

"What are you drawing your right leg up like that for?" he asked.

"Because it feels better that way. If it'd help I'd sit like a Yogi worshiper."

"Appendicitis, all right," he said. "Get Lula to fix you an ice bag and we'll run you in to the hospital this afternoon about six. We'll put you through the lab tonight, and, if indicated, operate in the morning."

"You'll do it, won't you? Albert may be all right, but I don't want any spriggins probing around in my guts."

"Yes…if you insist. I must tell you though, when I come out of retirement my fees are stiff."

"The hell with it," she said casually as she sat up grimacing when a twinge struck her. "I could buy you three times over and

sell you at a loss … in fact if I did sell you it would be at a loss."
She guffawed loudly and pushed a button on the table near her
couch.

A plump yellow Negro girl came to the door.

"Fix me an ice bag, Lula and don't be all day about it … I'm
dying. Bring another bottle of Coca Cola. This old bastard will
want a highball I know." Lula bowed and departed grinning
behind her hand.

"Do you have to revile me before the help?" reproved the
doctor mildly.

He made an undignified, unprofessional face at her and
ducked through the door to escape a bedroom slipper thrown
with deadly accuracy. As he went down the spiral steps he caught
a glimpse of Lula as she dashed across the hall into the servants'
quarters in the rear. She had been bathing and was only about
half clothed.

His beard moved up and down rapidly. "Not bad," he mur-
mured to himself.

Jeff Salton sat with Toni on the broad verandah and watched
the tree tops change color as the sun sank lower over the Mississippi.
The world seemed touched with a light crimson dust and the atmosphere was warm and quiet. From the living room there came the
hum of conversation telling of one of Lavender's teas.

"Your stepmother is in her glory," said Jeff, saltily.

Toni compressed her lips and looked away and Jeff sighed
heavily. She faced him suddenly.

"This has been very bad for you, Dad. I …"

"You couldn't help what happened, Kitten, and it has been
kept very quiet."

"Who'll ever believe I didn't just get caught like many another
girl?" she said bitterly. "And I'll bet you it has been talked about,
this very afternoon in there." She indicated the living room with
a limp hand.

"It better not be," Jeff scowled and gripped the stem of his pipe harder.

In the living room Lavender was indeed giving her friend Agatha Silvers an earful.

"It is such a warm thing to have a friend like you, Agatha. We don't see enough of each other ... really."

Agatha flushed with pleasure. "That's sweet of you. We'll have to do better. Now, my dear, I've been just simply bursting to ask you about Toni. I've been hearing all sorts of things ... ."

Lavender turned up her palms and sighed off a ton of weight from her chest. Her eyes were tragic and dismal. "Please ... too, too terrible. I couldn't talk about it. Really, to think that a Patterstall should ever ... but I can't go on, I simply can't!" She dabbed at her eyes with a wisp of a handkerchief.

"Oh, my dear," sympathized Agatha, leading her to a chair. "I didn't mean to make you sad ... how terrible it must be for you." She snorted and looked toward the verandah. "The Saltons always so high and mighty, too. Well, you never can tell. The girl's mother was one of those ... French ... or Creoles or something ... like mother like daughter, I always say."

Lavender nodded silently and turned her face away, the more effectively to suffer without any strain.

"Why, Lavender! Whatever put that stripe on your leg?"

Lavender jerked about and snatched her dress down where it had crept a little high disclosing a long livid mark. "Nothing at all," she said so sharply that Agatha started involuntarily. "Nothing really," said Lavender with greater calm. "I'm so tender, you know ... an old Patterstall trait. I scraped my leg on a projection on that old cherrrywood bed of mine. Now tell me, Agatha, what is the news? I haven't heard anything for a week."

Agatha's eyes gleamed and she lowered her voice confidentially. "Well, did you know that old man Chester's colored mistress had another boy ... that makes eleven boys and they are all the image of their father."

"I can't understand it," said Lavender. "The Chesters are some of the best people in the South."

"Humph, if you think that's bad, let me tell you! One of the Bell boys is right now living in the flats with a brown girl … living with her, I tell you. They never come out unless a flood runs them out, or they need groceries or something. I'll tell *you* if any kin of *mine* ever pulled such a stunt, they'd rue the day. I've asked Henry and he says he can't understand this weakness so many white men have for Negro girls. It's terrible!"

Lavender almost laughed. Henry might not be able to explain the anomaly but he had experienced it and Agatha was too dumb to know it or pretended it wasn't so. Lavender had it from the best sources that Henry and Charlie Chester had almost come to blows because Henry was paying too much attention to Charlie's oldest daughter by his dusky mistress. Henry had threatened to shoot Chester if he interfered and Chester being an arrant coward had retired in bad grace to growl and threaten.

Agatha chattered on for half an hour and exhausting her store of dirt, left.

Lavender sat in the dim light of the living room and stared unseeingly at the wall. The sun had set and the old house was as quiet as a tomb. Occasionally she could hear the faint clatter of a pan as Granny Rosa and the new girl cooked supper.

She stroked the welt on her leg with a curious avidity. What if Jeff had a colored woman that he was sleeping with? The thought struck her and rage foamed up. She had no proof but she was suspicious. If she ever caught him…. She got to her feet and stalked out into the wide hall and back to the kitchen. Enticing smells wafted through the open door to meet her as she approached.

"Rosa?"

"Yassum."

"Come out here on the porch for a minute. I want to talk to you."

Granny came through the door wiping shreds of biscuit dough from her hands with a dish towel. She took her pipe from her mouth and beat the ashes out on the heel of her hand.

"Rosa, who's the new girl?"

"She mah grandotter. Name Ge'aldine Cancer Jones."

"Good gracious, what a ridiculous name!"

"Yassum. She got a twin livin' wid me. She name Hilda Coppercawn. I give dem gals all dem names. Got 'em outa geography."

"Oh … Capricorn and Cancer … the tropics …"

"Yassum, dat's whut I sed."

"Well, what's the matter with Odele?"

"She in a fambly way."

"Yes, I seem to remember … however, it seems that a handsome girl like … er … Geraldine would get married."

"She ain't ready yit."

"Hummm. To tell you the truth, Rosa, I don't know that I like having such a girl as that about the house. You know men," Lavender tried to smile, but Granny's gimlet-eyed stare made it difficult. "Might make a man like Mr. Jeff get ideas … you see what I mean?"

Granny eyed her steadily. "Ef a man git whut he want in his own bed, he don't go pirootin' roun' lookin' fer nuthin' else."

Lavender flushed scarlet. "Why … Well, I never. … Do you mean to say that *I'm* at fault if he goes hunting on his own?"

"No'm," said Granny calmly. "Dat ain't what I *sed*."

"But you meant that."

"How come you thinkin' 'bout de boss. Whut 'bout Mr. Lem?"

She flushed again and her breathing became labored. "Lemuel can take care of himself and he isn't married. I must say, Rosa, that for a servant you take great liberties."

"You stahted de tawk," Granny pointed out with caustic logic. "An' enny time you wants to git yo' own cook in dat kitchen, you kin do it … leastways long's she keeps outen mah way when

I'm cookin' vittles fer de boss an' mah Sugar Baby." With that, Granny turned and waddled back in the kitchen, picked up a bell and rang it lustily to announce that supper was ready.

"I think," said Lavender, at the supper table, "that we should get another girl."

"What's the matter with Geraldine?" asked Jeff, ladling out heavy cane syrup on his hot buttered biscuit.

"Well, she's sort of quiet..." Lavender realized immediately that she must sound silly.

Jeff chuckled, "That, in my book, is a virtue of no mean caliber. I'd keep her for that reason if for no other."

"Well, I don't want her here."

Jeff was nettled. "Indeed, and what are your reasons? Certainly you aren't silly enough to want to get rid of a girl just because she's quiet."

Lavender lost her temper. "Isn't the fact that it is my desire enough? Haven't I, your wife, some say in the running of the house?"

"I seem to remember that you turned that chore over to Granny soon after you came here with cheers."

Lavender seemed to choke. "Then you won't send her away?"

Jeff shook his head. "That'll make Granny angry and I wouldn't want to do that."

Lavender leaped to her feet. "Then it *is* true... you *are* in love with her." She flinched as she realized that she had said the wrong thing and the blood receded from her face leaving it an ugly white.

Jeff slowly placed his knife and fork on his plate and folded his hands in his lap. His hard eyes almost beat her back into her chair and she started weeping into her handkerchief. "So," his voice was silky soft, "it finally came out."

"Really, Jefferson, I..."

"Oh, my God!" Toni rose to her feet. "You make me positively ill. What if he is in love with her? What have you done to prevent it?"

Jeff's heart leaped within him. At least Toni's revulsion toward things physical hadn't gone too deeply. "Sit down, Toni."

She put down her knife and fork. "No thank you."

"Henceforth," he told Lavender, who sat white and stricken in her chair, "scenes like this will be confined to some other part of the house. You've ruined Toni's supper and you've given me indigestion. This particular scene will not be repeated *anywhere*. I'm not in love with Geraldine and she stays."

Lavender got up slowly and went dispiritedly out into the darkness of the hall. He could hear her feet on the stairs. Lem came into the dining room with a muttered greeting and sat down and began to wolf food. He wasn't drunk as he usually was at this time of the evening and Jeff looked him over. "Where've you been, Lem?" he asked conversationally.

The other gave him a quick furtive glance and lowered his eyes again. "Oh ... looking around, walking around ... nothing."

Jeff grunted and began to pack his pipe. Geraldine came in quietly and her soft liquid brown eyes sought his with calm contemplation and held them for a moment. Instantly he knew she had heard what had been said at supper. It gave him an odd feeling of exultance and his own eyes remained steady. She turned away and began to stack the dishes. Lemuel watched her as she moved about, not missing anything. His heavy tongue licked thick sensuous lips and Jeff saw green glints deep in his eyes. When Geraldine went out with a load of dishes, Jeff said, "See something you like?"

The other started guiltily, muttered something unintelligible beneath his breath and attacked his supper again.

Jeff eyed him for a long time, then rose to his feet. "You," he said, transfixing Lemuel with a stiff forefinger, "had better be a good boy. I promise you, you'll be sorry if you don't." He walked out on the verandah where Toni sat curled up like a ball on the glider.

He sat beside her and she sat up to lean on his chest and hug him around the neck. "I'm sorry about that, Dad. She's a bitch...horrid."

He held her close and stroked her smooth back. "It's all right, Kitten. She won't do it again."

"But it was so snide—so uncalled for."

He nodded gravely. "Uncalled for, certainly, but understandable. Alcide could probably put it better, but here's what initiated it. She realizes, as you pointed out at the table, that she has done little to—well, she hasn't been much of a wife, physically speaking. Apparently, she can't. It's just not in her. She was an old maid too long, or I wasn't the swain I should have been. She resents that fact even though she can't do anything about it. She realizes the possibility that I might go in search of what she hasn't been able to provide. She won't provide nor would she allow me to attend to my biological needs elsewhere."

Toni looked him in the eyes. "You go right ahead and attend to your biological needs. Don't let that dried-up bud stop you, the vinegary old bitch!"

"Here, here. Let's not be disrespectful. She is your step-mother, you know...."

Toni flounced about on the glider. "I could kill her. She's no mother of mine." She stopped suddenly, her breast rising and falling rapidly to the spur of some emotion. She collapsed on his chest. "Oh, God, Pop, *I want my mother!*"

The pressure in Jeff's chest was almost unendurable. Quick hot tears stung his eyes and his throat worked as he tried to swallow the lump. Tears dripped on Toni's hands, making her look up, instantly contrite. "Oh...I'm so sorry. I shouldn't have said that."

"You do need your mother, Kitten...and I need her, too." Father and daughter held each other close and wept. Shedding tears for the dead but still revered Antoinette, the kind, the understanding, the beautiful.

CHAPTER SIX

BULL FALLON WALKED PROUDLY along the road toward Granny Rosa's house. There was a lithe swagger to his stride and he whistled a tune that finally broke into a song.

Gon' tell mah Mammuh … uh … uh
Bulldog done broke his chain—

His heavy bass voice broke sharply in the approved blues ending and echoed from the tall pines flanking the woods road. He had seen Hilda Capricorn the day before on the way to the store and Hilda had openly admired him. "Hi ya, gal," he had greeted her.

"Good evening," she had replied quietly.

"Wheh you been?" She had an armload of groceries which made it obvious, but Bull was making talk.

"I've been to the store."

"You talks like a gal whuts been to school!"

"I have."

"I ain't never went no further'n de third grade."

"That's a shame. Everybody ought to finish high school at least."

"Couldn't. I had t' wek in de fiel'. I gits along, though," he added proudly.

"You're big and strong. I'll bet you could really do some work."

Bull swelled mightily. "Ain't a hand in dis pa'ish whut kin keep up wid me."

"Well, I got to be going," she said. "These packages are getting awful heavy."

"I got to be going too," he said regretfully. "Got to git dese fo' plow pints shahpened down to de blacksmith shop. Wisht I wuz goin' back. I'd tote dem rations fer you."

Hilda Capricorn smiled showing strong white teeth. "Glad I saw you. Maybe I'll see you again some time."

Bull had bellowed laughter and swung his shoulders. "Ain't no way you kin keep frum it."

They had laughed, had gone their respective ways. Bull was now keeping his promise. The sad tune changed. The whistle again gave way to full throated words delivered with a deep blue refrain.

"Ummm ... ummmmm, ain't got no mama now.
Told me late las' nigh ... ite
Didn' need no mamma no how."

"Shet up singin' dat reel in frunt o' mah house, you deh, Bull. Gwine straight t' hell when you dies if you don' straighten yo' ways."

Bull laughed deep in his cavernous chest. "Tek mo'n dat t' sen' a man t' hell, Sis Rose. Wheh dat sharp-lookin' chicken gran'dotter o' yourn?"

"Come on in, boy," said Granny Rosa in a kinder voice. "She in de back somewhere. How's all?"

"All's well ... how's all wid you?"

"Tollable ... tollable. Nuthin' t' squall 'bout. Wheh you been keepin' yo' self?"

"Wekin'. I'se a hard wekuh, Sis Rose."

"Nacherly, you is. Yo' paw wuz a worker befo' you *and* yo' mammy. I hyeerd de boss say ef he hadda place full o' hands like you, he'd set on de gall'ry and tek root."

Bull began to swell. "Ef ever'body weks, den ever'body gits along. Us gits mo' and de boss gits mo'."

"Dat's de gospel," said Granny, smiting her meaty thigh. She turned in her chair. "Coppercawn, git sumpn' on an' come out hyer. You got cump'ny."

In a few moments, Hilda came out on the porch. She was dressed in cool white sharkskin and Bull's pulse hammered heavily. She was the most beautiful thing he had ever seen in the female form.

"Whooie," he sang. "Well done Jesus, Sis Rose. Dat gal fitten."

"Sho she is," said Granny, pleased immeasurably. "You oughta seed me when I wuz a shoat."

Bull gallantly pulled up a chair for Hilda and assisted her to sit. "Thank you, Mr. Fallon," she said formally.

"You is twict dat welcome," he said, not to be outdone in matters of form. "Hit wuz a stomp down pleasuh."

"Thank you, Mr. Fallon, you're very nice."

"Jools to de queen and candy to de kids," he shot back instantly. "Things whut come easy ain't no pain. Anything you wishes, you can have."

"Oh, y'all shet up all dat 'lasses tawk," growled Granny. "Soun' like a coupla white folks."

"Mr. Fallon is a very gallant gentleman, Granny."

Granny snorted and fingered a pinch of tobacco from a package of Red Tag and stuffed it in her pipe. "Well, I'se goin' t' bed," she announced. "Den, y' all kin play all de highfalootin' you wants to. Be keerful wid dat big buck," she told Hilda with a sharp glance. "His pappy wuz a demon wid de wimmen and I hear tell ... well, I ain't one to pack tales but you be keerful."

"I'll treat her like de fines' Dusbin china, Sis Rose," said Bull gallantly.

Granny snorted and stalked into the house.

"You mean Dresden china, don't you, Mr. Fallon?"

He waved a deprecatory hand. "I reckon so. I never could git dem Affykin names."

"But Dresden isn't in Africa, Mr. Fallon."

"Wheh it at?"

Hilda doubled up with laughter. "You really are priceless, Bull, no foolin'."

Seeing that she wasn't laughing at him too critically he joined in the laughter.

An hour later, they were seated in the swing in the full glare of a brilliant moon. Bull found himself examining her repeatedly from her trim ankles encased in white strap sandals upward past her fine husky calves to the shape of her round firm thighs outlined under the material of her dress. Her legs and hips blended smoothly and flowed gently, curving toward her small waist where the dress was secured by a green sash. Her breasts were high and full and they surged against the tight cloth in a manner which made Bull's mouth flush with a sudden freshet of saliva. The dress was cut low and the creamy valley, thus revealed, made him want to kiss her throat and work gradually downward. He placed an arm against the back of the swing and said huskily, "I ain't never seen a woman whut gits next t' me like you does."

She smiled gently and rubbed a cheek against his bulky shoulder. "You're kind of nice, too, Bull."

He sat up and making a half turn in the swing, faced her. "I c'n be a lot nicuh."

She put her head back against the swing and looked at him through deep slumbrous eyes. She smiled slowly and wrinkled her nose at him.

"Gawd," he breathed as he sank toward her. He found her lips expertly and proceeded to live up to the reputation he had inherited from his father. When he released her, she was starry-eyed and breathless. She ran a red tongue over her bruised lips, her body shuddering slightly at some powerful emotion.

"Bull ..." her arms became bands of steel and dragged him back into her embrace. This time it was Bull who was left gasping and dizzy.

He gazed cautiously at the open door. "If Sis Rose wuz to come through dat door rat now, I'd tek dat fence like a rabbit."

Hilda got up and flounced to the edge of the porch where she gazed upward at the moon and stretched. Bull followed her, stretching also. The dress rose, showing several inches of sturdy thigh and Bull squeezed his eyes shut and shook himself. This was maddening. She turned to him and reaching up, kissed him softly and quickly on the mouth. "If you really think I'm all that nice and if you're scared of Granny, it looks like you could think of something."

She had thrown the gauntlet down and Bull was on test. His mind moved like lightning. Alice was away at a quilting party and would be gone half the night. His house! That was the answer. He pulled her close and ran his hands lightly over her resilient back. He closed them about her waist and lifted her easily and kissed her. "You ax de questions, I got de answers .... Le's go."

When they arrived at the house the windows were dark and sightless. They mounted the porch and opened the door. For several seconds, the only sound was a slither of cloth then Hilda hurled herself at Bull with such force that it almost knocked him down. Gone was her educated veneer and to the ascendent came the hot blood of her savage forbears. Bull's nostrils dilated and his breath whistled as he, too, answered the call. Their writhing bodies came together in one mighty collision.

"How's Missy?" asked Maud, as Dr. Fontenot sat down to eat breakfast. He tasted his coffee before answering and smacked his lips appreciatively. "Fine. We operated last night because her white blood count was out of sight. She was bellowing like a bull this morning. Wanted to know if we intended to starve her to death and said if that was the case, why hadn't we let her die under the ether and save her the torment. She has all the nurses in stitches half the time and I had to take the other patient out of the room. Missy would have killed her in another day. The poor woman had had a cholecystectomy and Missy was about to kill her with ribaldries that'd make a statue die of mirth."

"When'll she be able to go home?"

"Oh, in a week or so, I guess."

Dr. Fontenot attacked his eggs with avidity and soon had his breakfast where it would do the most good. "Think I'll run over to see Toni Salton today. Might come back by Allen Gordon's and cast awhile for bass. Don't expect me till late. Oh .... er .... you wouldn't be one of Missy Blumendahl's stooges, would you?"

Maud eyed him woodenly and said nothing.

"Ummm, well just thought I'd ask. You women ...." He stalked from his house and got in his car.

Dr. Fontenot accepted a highball from Geraldine and as he did so, he gave her a quick searching glance. As far as he could tell, Cancer was as like Capricorn as the lines on the map indicated. "Where's Toni, Jeff?"

Jeff removed his pipe from his mouth. "She's still resting. I have insisted that she not get up until she has to."

"Good idea. Anything happen I ought to know?"

"No ... oh, yes. She has picked up quite a lot of animation and she accused Lavender last night of dereliction as regards my biological needs. I think this revulsion of hers is merely a condition connected with that night. I don't think it runs too deep."

"That would be a break all right. Time and the right man will do the trick as I have said ... or did I say that?"

Jeff grinned, "You said part of it. It is grand of you to take all this interest, Alcide."

The other shrugged. "I am interested, Jeff. If I may be a little harsh on your parental propriety, I'm doing it because the girl is a delightful morsel and should not go to waste. Some deserving man must get her and in the proper shape for a happy life. To be married to your daughter in the present frame of mind would be probably the most exquisite torture you could imagine."

Jeff nodded. "A lot of the prudery has leaked out of me lately. I'm not offended. I think I'm just beginning to see just how many tentacles this business of sex has. It drove me to think, it drove some low bastard to attack my daughter, it drove Lavender to accuse me of being in love with a colored girl, it drives poor Feathers to chasing everything that might provide a moment's gratification. I've wondered if there is anything more powerful in the whole tapestry of our existence."

"If there is I haven't found it," said the doctor tasting his drink. "For every one you mentioned there are a hundred others."

Toni came out on the verandah and shook hands with the old man. "You should have seen that breakfast I just put away."

"I'm glad to hear it, my dear. You're looking very well. Jeff, take a powder. I want to talk privately with my patient."

Jeff's eyes slitted, he clenched his pipe between his teeth and walked through the house toward the kitchen.

"Now my dear," said the doctor in a kindly voice, "is there anything you want to tell me?"

She met his gaze calmly. "No, I guess not. Nothing's changed … nothing … I still can't stand the idea of …" She bent her head over and held it up with a hand while a sob welled up in her throat.

CHAPTER SEVEN

BULL FALLON SPOKE SHARPLY BUT absently to Laura, his big red mule. "Haw! You deh, you fas'-steppin' red bastud. Wheh you think you goin'?" Laura obediently hawed and stepped faster. The ground was in good shape and the sharp plowpoint made little subdued thudding noises as it sheared through grass roots. The furrow tumbled cleanly against the one previously plowed and Bull, one hand on a handle, maneuvered the point deftly past a small stump which he had been laying off to "grabble" out. "One o' dese days," he muttered, "Ah'm gonna ketch a plow pint in dat stump and bust a beam er sumpn. Reckon I'll grabble it out some day when it's too wet to plow."

Laura put her head down as they struck a spot which had been but recently converted from turf. Bermuda grass grew thickly here and plowing was harder. Her ears flapped forward and back in time with her strides and the point made a steady tearing sound in the tough roots.

"Woah," Bull pulled the plow backward and scuffed damp dirt from the point. "G'up." Again Laura took up her swift pace and Bull broke into exuberant song.

You got to treat yo' baby right
Treat 'er eve'ry night,
Er she won't be home when you calls.

Bull ceased his song and stopped his mule. He had seen a furtive movement at the headland where plum trees grew thickly.

He had the usual amount of suspicion of things half seen so he peered steadily at the spot. Hilda stepped around the edge of the plum thicket and walked toward him. Bull's big face split wide open in a mighty grin, his white teeth gleaming in the sun.

"Seen you, but I thought you wuz somebody tryin' to play shahp wid me."

Hilda walked up and handed him an earthenware jug full of fresh cool water. "I thought you might want a drink, Bull."

"I sho do. Alice oughta been hyer wid mah wateh fo' now." He threw the jug across his thick forearm and let the water gurgle into his mouth. He handed it back to her and wiped his mouth with his wrist. "Dat wuz jes' right. Much obliged."

She smiled at him with such brilliance that he felt his skin go all prickly. "Come hyer, gal," he said huskily. She came to him obediently and he dropped his plowlines over the handles to have both hands free. He pulled her close with a jerk. His hands kneaded the firmness of her back muscles and he looked into her eyes.

"Day time is a bad time," he said breathing heavily.

She smiled and nodded happily. He could feel the warmth of her stomach against his own and the hard pressure of her breasts. He stepped back and shook himself.

"Dis ain't breakin' no ground," he said harshly. "Much obliged f' de wateh."

"Will I see you tonight, Bull?"

He laughed deep in his throat. "You bettuh not be seein' nobuddy else."

He slipped the loops of his lines over his wrists and hurled a hook into Laura's flank with the plowline that made her jerk. She leaped ahead with the trace chains crashing and the hames on her leather collar creaking. As they turned at the headland, Bull again thought he saw the figure near the plum trees. He frowned as he heeled the caked dirt from the plowpoint. He could see Hilda walking with her free long-legged stride along the terrace of the opposite hill. It couldn't be her. Bull made a decision. He'd investigate the next time he neared the plum thicket.

As they drew abreast of the thick growth of plum and black-berry briar, he pulled Laura to a halt and strode belligerently toward the thicket. "Whoeveh you is, come on out fo' I comes in deh and gits you." There was no sound so Bull ducked low to avoid the thorny low limbs and went in. Children picking plums had worn the ground smooth within the enclosure and the leafy walls made a pavilion of the growth. Bull straightened up and pulled a yellow plum from a low branch and popped it into his mouth. He spat out the seed and hull and reached for another but his hand never touched the fruit. There, sitting on his haunches not twenty feet away sat a great police dog which he recognized all too well. He whirled about with every intention of crashing to safety through the leafy wall that so effectively screened the tableau from the outside but there, as he had expected, stood Feathers. Her oblique green eyes burned with a restless fire and her face was cut with lines of intense desire.

"If you try to run, King will cut you to pieces," she told him. His great shoulders slumped dejectedly. He was beaten and he knew it.

When Alice arrived at eleven thirty with Bull's dinner, she found Laura unhitched, standing in the shade eating her corn. Bull lay stretched out on the ground nearby, drenched with sweat.

"You fell in de bayou?" asked Alice innocently.

"No ... I ain't fell in no bayou 'cause deh ain't no bayou t' fall in," snarled Bull rudely sitting up and mopping his face with a trembling bandanna.

"How come you so je'ky? You looks like sumbuddy run you fer ten miles."

Bull eyed his sister with smoldering hostility. "You," he said with slow distinct accents, "kin set dat vittles rat deh under dat gum tree. Den you kin turn roun' and go home jes' as strate as you feets kin go."

Alice eyed him for a space, then put the food down. "You sho is gittin' tetchy dese las' few days. Eveh time I opens mah mouf to you, you spews up like a bottle o' sour sorgum 'lasses."

Bull sighed heavily. His sister was something of a gossip and a trial. At such times as this, she was well nigh unendurable. He picked up his dinner pail but his hand was shaking so badly that he set it down again quickly. Alice, seeing that Bull was likely to get violent in his efforts to get rid of her, turned about and started for home. "Don't fergit n' leave dat bucket in de fiel'. Hit's de las' one us got."

Bull grunted and watched her out of sight. He glanced at the plum thicket and wondered if Feathers had gone. He fervently hoped so. Something would have to be done about her but though he pondered and scratched his head, he could think of nothing. Should he tell the boss…. He quailed at the thought. The boss was a good man, he knew, but white people were a little crazy where their women were concerned. What would the boss's reaction be if he knew.

Bull shuddered and yanked the top off the pail. Alice hadn't punched holes in the top and the hot rice and biscuits had sweated against the sides of the pail. The biscuits were soggy and the rice was wet. There were three huge slices of sowbelly there that looked good so Bull shoved a bite into his mouth and crunched down on it. Taking up his spoon he shoveled rice and gravy behind it and took a bite from a big red tomato. The cornbread was soggy too, but it went well with the collards. He finished the rice and gravy, collards and the sowbelly, then broke his last six biscuits and a square of cornbread into the bottom of the pail and poured on a half pint of thick cane syrup. He mixed it all together with his spoon and soon had the pail clean. As he finished, he looked up and there was the boss astride Big Red, looking down at him and grinning.

Jeff had a way of catfooting about and sneaking up when least expected. He had seen a lot by just such tactics that he never would have otherwise. Bull grinned guiltily as it was just twelve o'clock and he was supposed to work till twelve. He could hear the plantation bell ringing in the distance.

"Get hot, today, Bull?"

The big man glanced self-consciously at his drenched clothing. "Yassuh." This should be a good excuse for stopping early. "Sho is hot today. Hottes' day...."

"That's funny," Jeff interrupted. "Laura doesn't seem to mind it too much."

Bull hung his head. He was caught. Laura was not a heavy sweating mule to begin with and today she didn't even have her usual wet ring around her neck where she had sweated under the collar and a streak along her belly. He felt a sudden urge to confide in the boss but his blood turned to water and he remained silent.

Jeff dismounted and let Big Red crop the grass that grew thickly in the shade of the tree. "What was Feathers doing around here this morning?"

He darted a quick glance at Jeff.

"You seed her?"

Jeff nodded, careful not to seem too interested. "I thought maybe she was looking for me." Out of the corner of his eye, Jeff saw the hurried but searching glance Bull cast in the direction of the plum thicket.

"But tell me about it," said Jeff quietly.

Bull's chin touched his breastbone in an agony of indecision and consternation. Finally he sat straight and looked Jeff full in the eyes. "Boss, you got to help me."

"What's wrong?"

"Hit's. ... Miss Feathers." Bull spat on a forefinger and held it to heaven. "Hope Gawd strack me daid rat hyer in front o' you, Mistuh Jeff. ... I don' mess roun' wid white peoples. But one night I run into John Harrel's ole house t' git outa de rain and she wuz deh. I tried to jemp outa de winduh but she put dat big dawg on me. Ever'time I'd tried to git out dat dawg 'ud growel at me. I couldn't git loose, Mistuh Jeff, Gawd knows I couldn't." Bull's face screwed up dismally and great hot tears rolled from his eyes. "I hope Gawd'll strack me daid in mah tracks ef I ain't tellin' de Gospel."

Jeff placed a sympathetic hand on Bull's knee. "I know, Bull. She got me once."

A sobe of relief welled from deep within him. If she had got the boss, then he knew what it was like. "Sho nuff?"

"She sure did. I know just what you went through with ... but my God, she must have handled you rough."

Bull shrugged and rolled his eyes. "She might nigh kilt me bofe times. I ain't never seen a woman like her in mah bawn days."

Jeff swung up on Big Red. "Keep your eyes open and if you see her trying to get at you, come to me."

"Yassuh, I sho will but dat woman too smaht. Bofe times she had me fo' I knowed she was around."

"Well, do the best you can and I'll try to think of something."

"Yassuh," he broke out in a cool sweet sweat of unutterable relief. He had known all the time that the boss would understand ... and *he* had been caught too. There was something comical about that and Bull let a rumble of laughter seep from the depths of his chest. It was easy to laugh now because the world had taken a definite turn for the better.

He stood up and stretched. It was interrupted at the peak of satisfaction and he almost broke into a run when he heard a noise behind him. He whirled about and was immeasurably relieved to see the fat shapelesss form of Lemuel standing there.

Bull grinned amiably. "Mawnin' Mr. Lemuel."

Lem hiccoughed and lurched nearer. "I saw that fine-looking girl here that brought you water this morning." His grin grew wider.

"Fine as a fawty dollar cow, ain't she?"

Lemuel looked up slyly, "Sure she is, and I want her."

Bull stood stock still while icy waves flickered through his muscles. His fingers twitched as he swallowed a flare of raw fury. For a second, Lemuel was not a white man or a black but just a man who had evidenced a desire for Bull's woman. "Want and be goddamned!" hissed the Negro through his teeth. He paused appalled at his temerity while Lemuel grinned crookedly.

"Talk big, don't you?"

"I begs yo' podners, Mr. Lemuel," he said quietly, "I forgot who I was tawkin' to."

"Well, see that you don't forget again. I repeat I want that girl and you're going to get her for me."

Bull strove manfully to hold his temper, his black eyes turned bloodshot from the effort. "Don't tawk like dat t' me, Mistuh Lemuel."

Lemuel sneered, "I'll talk to you any way I want to. Now listen to me. You know John Harrel's old house? Well, I want her there tonight and you'll talk her into it."

The man's teeth showed whitely against the black skin and his great hands clenched murderously as he took an ominous step forward. Lemuel backed up rapidly. "Or I'll tell them what I saw in the plum thicket this morning. . . . I was right there and when I tell them about it in town, you know what'll happen to you. I'll expect her tonight." Lemuel turned and shuffled rapidly away.

Bull sank on the ground and shuddered with black despair. He was ruined and that was all there was to it. The boss . . . that was it. He held his head up. The boss . . . he'd know what to do. Bull leaped to his feet and with a swift motion he wrapped his lines about the hames and leaped on Laura. She took off toward the plantation house with a fast mincing pace.

He rapped her a sharp blow under the belly with a plowline and Laura, unaccustomed to this rough treatment, promptly kicked backward with enough force to burst the planking on the barn.

He patted her apologetically on the neck and by the time they came through the lot gate, Laura with an eye on another feed was loping rapidly along, trace chains jingling like sleigh-bells. Jeff seated on the verandah with Lavender and Toni, leaped to his feet and growled out an oath.

"What's the matter, dear," asked Lavender in her usually sac-charine voice.

"Nothing," answered Jeff shortly as he gripped the pipe tighter in his teeth and leaped down the steps.

"I do wish your father would mend his ways of speaking to people," she complained. "It is so rude and boorish."

Toni let her violet eyes rest on her stepmother for a time, then looked toward the barn again. She said nothing.

Bull slid from Laura's back and when Jeff walked into the barn, he had the gear off the mule and was turning her into a stable.

Jeff walked up. "Not already, Bull." The man's stricken eyes told the story. "What's the matter?"

Bull sat down abruptly on a feed basket. "Ever'thing's de matter, boss." Then he told his story. Jeff sat very still and lis-tened. "I been a good man, boss. You knows dat. You had to pay de lawyer dat time Sis Tilly Bryant put de law on me dat time 'bout Sissy. But boss, Hilda is plumb differunt. Dat gal done got me and when Mr. Lemuel tole me to fetch her to dat ole house, I might nigh fergot I ...."

"Filthy son of a bitch," Jeff ground out, leaping to his feet. "Where is he?"

No answer was needed because at that moment, Lemuel loped into sight on a little pinto, the only horse on the place he'd ride. He rode into the barn, but coming into the dark building from the bright sunlight, he didn't see them till he had dismounted.

"Come over here, Lemuel," said Jeff.

Lemuel shrank back against a stable door. "Now look, Jefferson ... I ...."

With a bound Jeff covered the space between them and fastened his hand in Lemuel's shirt collar. He forced him back hard against the door and began to beat him about the face with hard bruising open-handed slaps. Lemuel screamed and struggled but in Jeff's mighty grasp, he was helpless. Jeff wore a huge graduation ring, a heavy hunk of metal that was cutting Lemuel's face to ribbons. With a surge of power Jeff pulled him away from the door and hooked a terrific right to the other's ear. It cracked suddenly and Lemuel crumpled to the straw-and-dung covered floor of the barn. Jeff breathed hard, looking at the prone figure. He took out the handkerchief and wiped the blood and saliva from his hands.

Bull sat riveted to the feed basket, numb with satisfaction. That's what happened to people that got sharp with the boss's Negroes.

Jeff turned to him. "Take the rest of the day off. You need it. You want to marry Hilda?"

Bull got slowly to his feet. "More'n I want to live. I'da never done what Mr. Lemuel said."

Jeff nodded. "Of course you wouldn't. You can go to town tomorrow and tell Sol Lehven to let you have what furniture you need. That stuff in your house is about to fall to pieces. You wouldn't want to bring a good girl like Hilda into a house like that. Tell Sid Wright I said to go over that house and put it in top shape. If you want a coat of paint on it, you can do it yourself. I'll give you the paint."

The Negro swallowed something that had risen in his throat. "Boss, I can't say it."

Jeff smiled and struck him on a hard shoulder with his fist. "Don't say it, then. We're grown men. We understand each other."

Lemuel had to be taken to the doctor. His face was cut deeply in a dozen places and was bruised to a wonderful shade of blue. Lavender immediately launched into a fit of hysterics and Granny Rosa had to put her to bed. Jeff refused to get into an argument about what had happened and there was nothing left to do but have hysterics. Toni strode off and left her so Granny dragged, rather than carried her to her room and left her.

When Lemuel was led into the room two hours later, she was composed and immediately jumped on him.

"Well…so now *you're* running after Negro women. You nearly got yourself killed for your trouble. What'll it be, next?"

Lemuel lay on the bed and sobbed into his bandages. "You made me like this," he was sobbing pitifully. "I was a normal man and you made me into one of those…those…creatures. I never wanted to be anything but what I was…you made me…made me." He sat up in bed and pointed an accusing finger at her.

"Shut up!" she blazed. "You were always as twisted as you could be. It was born in you like it was born in me. I don't know where you get this normalcy thing. You never did before we came here."

"I never wanted to, before we came here," he sobbed. "You never gave me a chance. You always made me do what you wanted and I never went against you, never. You shouldn't want me to not ever have any…any…anything of my own."

"I don't care what you have," she said harshly. "What I do care is that you are a fool. Look at what you just did. Have you no sense at all? Don't you know that Jeff Salton is quite capable of killing you? You and your threats! All they'll do is cause trouble for us. I hope you see that now."

Lemuel's sobs quieted a little and he did not speak.

The week following, Lemuel so effectively kept out of sight that Jeff could almost feel that he had gone. If some stroke of divine providence could have taken Lavender along too, everything would have been fine. He wondered if she would make good her threat to blacken Toni's name? What would he do if she did start poisonous whisperings?

Lavender had no such intention. If she could have by innuendo said something to let it out, she'd have done it already, but on that score she was more than satisfied. Her talk with Agatha Silvers had shown that the knowledge was abroad and she had, without saying anything directly, given support to the rumor. Agatha would now tell it as first hand information. Lavender was not a fool. She could see that beneath the good natured and easy going surface of Jefferson Salton, there was a streak of finely tempered steel.

At Fomalhaut she had a good thing of it. She was looked up to, socially, being a parishwide leader in all cultural and social affairs, and she enjoyed her position. She was not going to jeopardize it by any stupid obvious act. Whatever she did, she'd do it under cover.

It was three o'clock in the afternoon and Jeff rose from his afternoon nap feeling logy. The weather was abominably hot and his head ached slightly, a dull full feeling that resembled a hangover. He thought of a drink and put the thought from him. It was too hot to drink. Iced tea ... that was the thing.

He walked through the hall and back to the kitchen. Granny Rosa sat in a big rocker in the shade of a column and slept, her lips popping occasionally as she breathed.

In the kitchen, Geraldine was tending a big pot full of dish cloths which were undergoing their weekly boiling in strong lye water.

"Good evening, sir. Can I get you something?"

"Er—yes, Geraldine. I'd like some iced tea. Why don't you wait till dark to boil these things? It's too hot now."

She smiled. "I don't mind the heat, sir. It's the cold that gets me. I'll get the tea."

He sat on the little kitchen porch that was away from the sun and shaded by the branches of a live oak. It was cool and there was a little breeze.

Geraldine came back quickly with a tall frosted glass of tea and handed it to him. She hesitated for a moment and Jeff looked up. "You've worked in that kitchen long enough," he said with a smile. "Get yourself a coke from the ice box and come back here and rest a while in the cool."

She came back with a glass full of coke and ice and sat on the steps at his feet. He could see where the sweat had wet her simple gingham dress down the deep cleft of her strong back. Her hair was damp around the temples and extremely soft. Being conscious of her hair and proud of it, she had always paid it a great deal of attention. It was shoulder length and fell orderly in deep soft waves. Usually she had the bulk of it tied with a bit of colorful ribbon making it fit her face closely. This afternoon, being hot, she had it pulled closely back and above her ears. Jeff noticed that they were well formed and small, nestling close to her head.

"Mr. Jeff, you won't let them do anything to Bull, will you?"

"Not if I can help it, Geraldine. What Bull did was not his fault. Everyone knows that who knows anything about it. Bull wants to get married, I think."

"Yes, sir. My sister, Hilda, is so crazy about him, I think it would kill her if a mob got him."

"I think Lemuel is cured," said Jeff, his voice getting hard and angry lines showing on his forehead.

Geraldine shuddered at the mention of the name. "It gives me goose bumps when he looks at me."

Jeff was shaken by such a blast of rage that he nearly dropped his glass. "He hasn't done… made any moves toward you, has he?"

"Oh, no, sir," she said quickly. "I just don't like the way he looks at me."

"I don't blame you. I wonder why he picks on Hilda. You're here every day and anyone can see he has an eye for you, and you look just like her."

Jeff could see her fine tawny skin go dark under the wave of blood that mounted to her face. She remained silent. Suddenly he became curious. She knew something or she wouldn't have blushed.

"Geraldine...."

"Yes, sir?"

"What were you thinking about, just then?"

She turned her face away and a strange feeling came over Jeff. Suddenly it seemed important that she should know that she could tell him anything without reservation. He didn't want her to feel stiff and uncomfortable around him. Although the feeling startled him somewhat, he was too honest at heart to deny it or pretend it hadn't happened.

"Geraldine."

"Yes, sir."

"Why don't you tell me?" His voice was deep and gentle.

She faced him and he could see the effort she was making. "Please, sir, can ... you won't be angry at me if I tell you?"

He smiled his assurance and managed to look almost boyish. His clear eyes sparkled and goodfellowship shone from them. "I'm not an ogre. You've been here long enough to know that."

She swallowed and looked out across the green stretch of the lawn toward the bluff. "I don't really know why Mr. Lemuel hasn't ... you know ... but Granny says it's because...." She stopped and hung her head.

Jeff leaned over and placing one hand on her firm shoulder made her face him. "Yes?"

She looked him full in the yes. "Granny said she told Mr. Lemuel that I was yours and that if he bothered me, you'd kill him."

Jeff sat back, his strength suddenly snatched from him. His head whirled and maddening half thoughts fought for coherence. Honesty made him admit that this strange girl attracted him greatly but four thousand years of prejudice and white supremacy prevented him from making the final admission. As a result the effect was one of great confusion.

"You're not angry, Mr. Jeff?" she asked fearfully, anxiously.

He grinned weakly. "No, Geraldine. I'm knocked over, that's all."

He could see the thread of tension break within her and relief take its place. She put her hands up to her face and held them there for a long time. Jeff said softly, "It took a lot of courage to say that to me, didn't it?"

"Yes, sir, it took more than courage, Mr. Jeff."

He did not ask her what she meant by that, for the simple reason that he was afraid to.

"How did you feel when Granny told you she had told Lemuel that?"

She was silent for a while and Jeff began to wish he hadn't asked the question. "Mr. Jeff, I can't talk about that."

"Why, Geraldine?"

"Because it's too close to me ... it's ... ."

He made an attempt at lightness, feeling as he did so that he was going close to dangerous grounds. "Well, it's pretty close to me, too." Oh, Lord, he thought, I've done it now.

He had. She faced him quickly, her mouth slightly opened and her breath coming swiftly. "How is it close to you, sir?"

Again he attempted to be gay. He smiled widely. "Because I'm in it, too. I'm the one she scared him with."

"Oh ... ." Her voice was very small and far away. He felt that he had hurt her and he was afraid to analyze the extreme distaste which rose in him at the thought. White men did not bother to wonder or even care whether they hurt their colored retainers. Often they hurt them and never knew it because they never thought about the matter at all. His next remark showed how thoroughly he had been thrown off his course.

"I thought...the reason I asked you.... I thought maybe when Granny said that, you wouldn't have liked the idea of...being mine." He raged inwardly at his traitorous tongue.

She stood up, her dark mysterious eyes resting on his with upsetting directness.

"Mr. Jeff, you haven't asked me to be yours. Whenever you do, I'll be ready to answer you."

She turned swiftly away and disappeared into the kitchen.

CHAPTER EIGHT

B ULL FALLON LAY ON HIS CORN shuck mattress and tossed fitfully. He seemed nervous and fretful, which was something
entirely foreign to his nature. Usually he was asleep by the time
he had arranged himself comfortably but tonight he could not
sleep. He quit flouncing and lay very still so as to not arouse the
dry protest of the shucks which always made a great deal of noise
when he moved. Suppose Mr. Lemuel did tell off on him like he
had threatened? He sighed heavily.

Between Feathers and Lemuel he was in the hottest of water.
He shivered, thinking of the plum thicket episode. Never in
all his varied experience had he encountered such a woman as
Feathers. There had been several lynchings in the state during his
lifetime and he had a vivid recollection of each one.

The night outside was quiet and very dark. There'd be a
moon but not till after midnight. Insects by the thousand gave
out their cheepings and raspings. A sleeping mockingbird let fall
occasional trickles of melody and a great horned owl, up from the
flats on a raid, chuttered nastily a quarter of a mile away. A stick
snapped outside the house and Bull started nervously and sat up
in bed. His nerves quivered and all his senses seemed to become
abnormally sharp.

He heard a muttered word and another stick cracked. With
scarcely a sound, he slid from the bed and drew on his trousers.

Hilda and Geraldine lay on their bed clad in colorful pajamas. Geraldine was asleep but Hilda lay on her back and thought

about her man. Her body wriggled with the sensuous trend of her thoughts and her breath came a little faster. Outside the house on the main road, she heard the crunch of gravel. At first, she thought nothing of it until it seemed unduly prolonged, then she became curious. She slipped from her bed and crept to the front door, cracked the portal and peered out. A number of men were passing and most of them walked on the shoulder of the path to avoid the noisy gravel. Others didn't seem to mind, and she heard a smothered chuckle which was echoed by a drunken laugh.

A gruff voice spoke and the noise subsided. A match flared and she saw a sharp-featured white man apply the flame to a cigarette. She saw something else too. The man walking beside him carried a double-barreled shotgun.

Cold sweat broke out on the girl's amber skin and a sob caught in her throat, Scurrying back to their room she swiftly slipped from her pajamas and into a pair of Levis and into sneakers. She slipped a black pullover sweater over her head and silently crept out of the house. She followed the band of men until she was sure that they had gone to Bull's house, then she stopped to consider. What should she do? The same doubt assailed her that had caused Bull's hesitation on another occasion. Should she tell the boss?

In what way was he different from most white men except that all his hands seemed to think that he was the best boss in the parish? Hilda stood and squirmed in an agony of indecision. If she ran to the boss and he turned out to be of the same mind as the mob, she had made matters worse; if she didn't go to him, Bull hadn't a chance. She heard the mutter of hoofs behind her and leaped to the cover of a thicket of blackberry briars just in time to avoid a horse being ridden at a rapid pace. She couldn't tell who it was but as soon as it had passed, she came out into the little side road again. Suddenly she made up her mind. She'd tell the boss. Bull was certainly lost if she didn't, so she started toward the big house at a rapid dogtrot. She hadn't gone a hundred steps when a shotgun exploded ahead of her. She was cut off from the house and they were shooting at Bull now. She clutched her head in a frenzy of despair and moaned loudly, "Jesus, God … do something … *do* something."

Feathers took off her clothes and ran a cold shower in her rooms on the second floor of the old gray Maidstone house. Then she hurled herself across the bed still nude and lay supinely for a while. She sat up and gazed abstractedly out into the star-studded night. She thought of the dark night of the thunderstorm when she had caught Bull in John Harrel's old house. She lay slowly back and rolled sinuously on her back. Her eyes stared at the ceiling and in her mind she could feel again the strutted crush of his great muscles and the savage abandon of his thrusts, the strong masculine scent of his magnificent body. A light sweat broke out on her upper lips and forehead.

Some time later, Feathers came from the shower and stood in the window allowing a cool wind to touch her damp skin. On the porch below, she could see the dim forms of her mother and father as they sat and rocked silently. A man came up from the black shadows and addressed her father. She could hear snatches of the conversation.

"… and we think you oughta come along."

"Ah ain't never been with a mob in mah born days," she heard the rumbling drawl of her father retort, "and Ah don't aim to be now."

"I don't believe you know," said the man in wonderment.

"Know what?" asked Maidstone.

For a moment the man stood silently, then walked away into the shadows. A wave of horror swept over Feathers as the import of the last remark struck her. If her father had been sought to join a mob and the man thought it odd that he didn't know what for, then it could mean but one thing. They had found out Bull in some manner. With a pantherish spring, she leaped away from the window and slipped into her jeans. Dressed, she went to a closet and pulled out a slim automatic shotgun. Breaking open a fresh box of shells she began to cram them into her pockets.

King preceded her through the door and to gether, with the utmost caution, they descended the long winding stairs and went out the back door of the big house. Ten minutes later she mounted her red horse and trotted silently away, the heavy turf muffling the hoof beats ....

Two earsplitting explosions from a shotgun fired close to the house snatched Jefferson Salton from his bed with a jerk and before he was half awake, he had his pants and slippers on. The dull roar of many voices rose in the distance and he heard the sound of pounding feet coming nearer. With a bitter oath, he went to his dresser, took out two heavy Colt automatics and checked the clips. He worked cartridges into the chambers and thrusting them into the waistband of his pants, ran out of his room and down the stairs. As he came out on the verandah, Bull coming in a dead run almost knocked him down.

"Boss, dey comin' fer me," he panted raggedly. With a flip of his hand, Jeff switched on three powerful floodlights that turned the lawn into day. Some forty men in a straggling group came trotting across the lawn.

"Get back into the house, Bull," Jeff ordered. "Did they hit you?"

"Nawsuh—not bad. Jes' some birdshot under mah skin."

Jeff closed the door on him and walked to the edge of the porch to face the men.

"Good evenin', Mr. Salton," said Jasper Mutlock, evidently the leader of the group. His eyes were bleary and red. A quick glance showed Jeff that the whole group was more or less drunk.

"What do you want, Jasper?"

"We wants that big Bull what just run in here."

Jeff hefted the two Colts in his capable fists and looked the group over with unfriendly eyes. "You have two minutes to get off this place."

A murmur ran over the crowd but they made a noticeable mass retreat.

"We don't aim to have no trouble, Mr. Salton," said Jasper, careful not to get too far from the mass of his followers, "but we want that nigger."

"And I say you don't get him," said Jeff, his voice hissing between his set teeth.

"Jefferson, you come in the house this instant," shrilled Lavender from behind the door. "If they want the Negro, let them have him."

"Half your time is up," said Jeff, ignoring his wife. "You are trespassing on private property and...." The gun in his right hand thundered and Thad Berry screamed, grabbed his knee and sank to the ground. He had tried to take a bead on Jeff with a twenty-two rifle.

"Take him and get going," said Jeff. "The next one will get it through the head."

The men were silent for a moment, the only sounds being the whines of Thad begging someone to help him. A revolver cracked in the rear of the mob. Jeff swayed like a stricken pine and fell full length down the front steps, both guns going off as he fell. One bullet ricochetted off the live oak, a few yards away and went whining into the night. The other struck the stone flagging of the walk, ricochetted and nearly tore Thad Berry's head from his body. A deep silence fell that was broken by a roar from Bull as he leaped from the house to help his master.

Long and well did the mighty Negro strive and many were the bones that snapped under the awful drive of his mighty arms and his powerful legs, but gun butts are too hard and the men were too many and ten minutes after he had leaped among them, Bull was a bruised bloody hulk securely bound with insulated telephone wire and strapped like a gutted deer to a long pole by his hands and feet.

As the mob trooped away from the house bearing their dead and cripples, Hilda Capricorn sank to her knees and terrible sobs tore themselves like lacerating grapples from her heaving chest. Again she heard horses' hoofs, but this time they were rapid and staccato. She didn't care about horses now and Red Mack's agility saved her as he carried over her with a tremendous bound and snort. Feathers pulled the champing animal to a sliding halt and turned him around.

"What are you doing there," she asked.

"They got Bull," said Hilda numbly staring up at the straight figure of the girl on the horse. "You got him in this... why don't you get him out?"

Feathers looked at her for a moment. "I will," she rapped out and wheeling Red Mack on his haunches, she cut him under the stomach with her quirt and was gone. Hilda seeing the shotgun in her hands sobbed with relief and took out after her as fast as she could run.

Bull was tied to a young pine. He was only half conscious and his eyes were nearly closed from the terrific beating he had received. He could smell kerosene and felt its warm dry bite as Jim Hardt splashed it on his chest and legs. A droplet went in one eye and it began to smart but he was only slightly conscious of this last extra bit of pain. He breathed deeply and straightened his body against the tree. Thirty feet away, a huge fire roared redly. "I'll burn like that," he thought, "but I won't last as long."

Bull prayed that in some manner death would come quickly but he knew of these things. They didn't want it to come quickly. He looked the group over. Most of them he knew and all he knew were *buckrahs* ... po' white trash ... the kind you steered clear of in town on Saturday night ... the kind to whom the nebulous tenets of white supremacy were the only thing they had with which to feed their pride. The good white people, he remembered, looked down on the *buckrahs,* while the trash had no one to look down on but the Negroes. The bottle passed freely and Jasper Mutlock addressed his men in a thick voice.

"If we all 'lows 'em t' carry on with our women, what's this here country coming to? Somebuddy answer me that." No one answered him but a mutter of approval went through the crowd.

"This here is a white man's country," continued Jasper, "and if they are gonna take it over and rape our women, then we all had better move out."

"What we need," said another voice, "is the kluxers to come back."

"That's 'zactly right," said Jasper with heat, "and till they gits back we's the ones to take care of rapers."

"Who got raped?" asked Will Hadley as he sat some feet away watching the men through narrow lids. Will had talked against the lynching and Jasper wheeled on him.

"Miss Feathers, that's who, and if you don't like it here, why don't you gwan home?"

Will looked at Jasper for awhile. "That's a goddamned good idea."

He rose and walked away through the woods. He had hardly passed from sight when a shotgun thundered nearby and the whiskey bottle disappeared from Tom Sturgun's hands and most of it entered Zack Ellier's face, leaving it red and raw as a piece of beef. Zack screamed and fell backwards away from the fire, holding his face with both hands. Four more shots rang out and the men, bitten hard by bird shot, ran pellmell through the woods, followed by the hard hoofbeats of a running horse. Other shots rang out and other screams sounded through the tangled underbrush. Hilda rushed from cover and tore frantically at the wires binding Bull to the tree.

Finally he was free but he couldn't walk. He sank to the soft pine needles and began massaging his feet with hands that were little more than sticks, dead from lack of circulation.

Zack was crawling aimlessly in circles whimpering for some-one to help him, that his eyes were put out. Bull glared at him and picking up a pine knot bounced it expertly off his head. Zack yelled and lurched to his feet and finding that he was not as blind as he had supposed took off under forced draught through the woods.

By the time Bull had rubbed sufficient circulation into his legs to stand, Feathers was sitting on her horse on the other side of the clearing, watching them silently. Hilda looked at her with dumb gratitude notwithstanding the fact that it was primarily Feathers' fault that the trouble had occurred. Bull staggered a little as he tried to walk. "I sho thanks you, miss," he said, "I sho does."

Feathers looked steadily but said nothing. Finally she pulled Red Mack's head around and disappeared in the darkness.

"Got t' git back to de house. Dey shot de boss."

"Sure, honey, but take it easy. You can't walk good yet."

"Sho I kin walk," he said crossly and set out at a fairly good pace. He found himself tiring before long, however, and had to slow down.

"Honey, you don't have to show off before me. I know you're good when you're well but you have been beaten up something terrible. It's only good sense to take it easy."

He grinned a crooked self-conscious grin. "You's too smaht fer a woman. You reads people's minds."

She hugged him and made him slow down. They skirted the bluff and just before they came out into the open, Bull had to sit down.

"Mah head goin' round like a 'lasses mill," he complained holding the offending member with both hands. Hilda sat beside him.

"It'll be all right if you'll rest awhile."

But it grew worse and finally Bull passed out cold. Hilda then became frightened and started to go for help. She hadn't gone thirty feet into the clipped area of the lawn when she heard a noise. Turning with a gasp, she saw Lemuel leering at her. "So Bull wouldn't help me out, eh? Well, now, isn't that tough. Look where he is now?"

Hilda said nothing but stood still watching his slow approach. "I won't need Bull now," he continued. "I can get along without him. You and I can be good friends."

"Don't put your hands on me, Mr. Lemuel."

His lips curled, "I'm not asking, Hilda. I'm taking!"

He grasped her roughly about the waist and pulled her to him. With a serpentine twist, Hilda tore away and slapped him a resounding blow in the face. Lemuel lost his temper, lunged at and threw her roughly to the ground. Even then, she might have been a match for him but Lemuel had no intention of losing this battle. When he saw that the struggle might go against him, he scrambled to his feet and as she came up, he struck her twice in the face almost knocking her over the edge of the bluff. He pulled her back, half conscious, and calling for Bull in a weak voice.

"No damn good…to call him…he won't…come." He deliberately struck her again on the point of her chin and she sagged limply, unconscious. A cackle of laughter came from him as he fondled her breasts and tore at her clothing. So rapt was he in his own intentions that he went high in the air and over the edge of the bluff without ever knowing what agency caused his soaring flight.

At the bottom of the bluff some seventy feet down was the body of an old car with two windshield uprights pointing drunkenly at the sky. Falling the entire distance, Lemuel was spitted like a roasting fowl on one of those uprights with eighteen inches of it protruding through his fat belly. Bull was bending over Hilda and scarcely heard the tinny crash that came faintly from below.

When they reached the house, it was ablaze with lights. Geraldine and Granny Rosa darted hither and thither at Toni's

ragged their weary feet up the steps to the
back porch near the kitchen.

"De boss ... he hurt bad?" he asked Granny as she bustled up.

"Don't know. Dr. Fontenot and dat boy doctor o' hisn on
their way hyer now. How you got 'way frum dem peoples?"

"Miss Feathers saved him, Granny. She shot men as long as
there was any to shoot."

"She sho did dat," agreed Bull, nodding.

"Gawd bless de Fillystines," squeaked Granny in stunned
amazement. "Whut goin' happen round hyer nex'?"

"Us gon' git ma"ied," said Bull proudly.

Granny sniffed and disappeared into the kitchen. Her voice
floated back to them, "Better! Else funny thaings gon' be comin'
round hyer ... if y'all don' watch out."

Bull and Hilda stole a cautious glance at each other and Bull
shook his head, grinning, "Dat ole 'oman ...."

Dr. Fontenot placed a tender hand on Toni's shoulder.
"Nothing to worry about, child. The bullet was small ... a thirty-
two, I think. Just grazed the skull a few inches and knocked him
silly. What is that other pool of blood near where he was shot?"

Toni shuddered. "When he fell his guns went off and one
bullet hit a man in the head and ...."

"Never mind," interposed the little man. "I saw the place ... I
know. Too bad he didn't have a tommygun in each fist and could
have got the whole crowd. Poor Bull. He was a fine fellow to have
around."

"I'se still here, too," said Bull, putting his grinning face
through the door.

Toni spun around and gasped.

"Sacré nom du mort. He's still alive. Well, devil my liver!"
whistled the doctor.

"Sho is," said Bull, sidling into the room. "Kin I see de boss, please suh?"

Dr. Fontenot waved his hand. "There he is, in good shape. I've got him asleep now, but he'll be all right.... Albert, don't take all night with that dressing. We've got to get back some time tonight."

Albert put on two more strips of tape and stood up. "Excellent job, even if I do say to myself."

"Nuts," said his father rudely. "I could have done better in half the time."

Toni caught them by the arms as they went out. "I don't know how to thank you two. I called you sort of automatically even though there are other doctors nearer."

"A natural desire for the best," said Albert laughing. "We understand and when you get our bill, you might want to take back them kind words."

Toni sat on the verandah and watched Dr. Fontenot and Albert disappear around the curve of the long driveway. It was late but Toni did not feel like sleep, rather like a deer that had escaped the hunters after a long hard chase. She smiled grimly at the thought. Bull was the one who should feel like the escapee. He and Hilda had disappeared arm in arm after Dr. Fontenot had examined him and found no serious injuries.

Toni sighed. Bull and Hilda seemed as carefree as though the attempted lynching hadn't occurred. She wished she could shake herself loose from the strangling fingers of her own trouble. She was intelligent enough to know that her chances for happiness with her present fixation were nothing to speak of. She recalled the night, the animal-like relish she had felt with the cold rain pelting down on her bare skin and the abrasive joy of the rough bath towel. Abruptly she changed the thought because it would progress to where she had awakened and felt the heavy body on her ... the heavy body with the sour smell.

She heard a quiet step behind her and turned around. It was Geraldine.

"Is there anything else I can do, Miss Toni?"

"No, thank you, Geraldine. I guess that's all. Pop's resting easily and I'll just sit here till I get sleepy."

"Why don't you let me fix you a stiff drink? It might make you sleep better."

Toni considered, then nodded. "That might be a good idea."

Geraldine disappeared and came back quietly with a highball. Toni took it and smiled her thanks.

"You might as well go on home, Geraldine. There isn't anything else … and thanks a lot."

"That's all right, Miss Toni, I was glad I could help." She stood uncertainly for a moment and Toni looked at her keenly. "Is there anything … ?"

"Yes'm. I don't think Mr. Jeff should stay in that room all alone. He might wake up and be out of his head or something."

"That's right. I'll …"

"No, please mam … let me stay. Mr. Jeff is always anxious for you to get all the sleep you can. You've had a bad night and I … well … I'm a lot stronger than you. I'll be glad to stay."

The tense urgency of Geraldine's voice penetrated, but Toni couldn't account for it. She searched the calm face as shown by the dying rays of the moon but there was only a certain breathless tension about the eyes. She wanted to stay … wanted very much to stay.

"Certainly, Geraldine. I'd appreciate it if you'd stay."

Geraldine ducked her head in a quick bow and turned away. For a long time Toni sat and sipped her drink, thinking. She put the empty glass on the floor and stood up. She was a little dizzy from the drink but she felt relaxed and sleepy. She took one last look out across the dimly lighted lawn where even the katydids had ceased their rasping songs, turned and walked into the house, still thinking about Geraldine. Why had she been so anxious to stay? Probably taking cue from the loyalty of her grandmother.

Toni undressed and slipped into a sleeping garment fashioned after a play suit. It was thin and cool and she now had a frightful aversion to sleeping nude. Previous to her experience, she had preferred to sleep in the raw but now she couldn't bring herself to do it. She also paid meticulous attention to the door which she locked every night.

She leaped into bed, flouncing like a fish on dry land, landing spreadeagled in her favorite position, her head half buried in a soft pillow and her limbs pointing to all points of the compass.

Involuntarily her mind wandered back to Geraldine. She *had* been very anxious to stay... she had been the first to find Jeff sprawled at the foot of the steps since Toni had unaccountably slept through the whole thing only half awakening when the shots went off, taking some ten minutes to fight her way to full wakefulness. The shotgun blasts had wakened Granny and Geraldine and they had gotten to the house before Toni was fully awake. She'd never forget that Geraldine had carried her father from the stone walk to the living room couch without help... alone she had carried him and Jeff was no small man.

A tiny bright light suddenly glowed in Toni's brain. Could she be in love with Jeff? The thought was such an edged one that Toni sat upright in her bed.

Well, what was there to prevent the emotion if the ingredients were present? She remembered Jeff's flustered look as he had come from the rear of the house the other day. Had he been to the kitchen? Was it an attraction to Geraldine that had made him flush so redly and say he had been thinking about a girl?

Toni thought of her acidulous stepmother and her lip curled only to smile with a certain devilish crinkling of her eyes. Given a choice between Lavender and Geraldine, what man could be blamed if he leaned toward the latter? A little ripple of laughter trickled from deep in Toni's chest and she slipped lithely from the bed and rammed her feet into a pair of bedroom slippers. Jeff's room was down the hall and to the left, just opposite Lavender's and Toni made for it with cautious soundless strides. There was a small table lamp which sent out a feeble fan of light through the door that stood several inches ajar.

When Geraldine came upstairs, she walked to the room and slid through the small opening in the door leaving it as it was, because it had a tendency to squeak and she didn't want to disturb the patient. She lifted a chair and placed it carefully near the head of the bed and sat down. She hitched it a few inches closer till she could peer directly into the face on the pillow. For a long time, she looked at him devouring every line in the placid face and conquered a desire to smooth the little laugh wrinkles at the corners of his eyes. She sat back and settled herself for the vigil.

Geraldine must have dropped off to sleep because Jeff's voice coming out of the night startled her and her eyes snapped open. He was looking at her with a queer fixed expression in his eyes.

"Antoinette, why aren't you in bed?"

Geraldine swallowed and felt a wave of cold flicker over her body. He thought she was his dead wife … he was living in the past. Bravely, she mustered her will. "I didn't feel sleepy," she said softly. "Go back to sleep."

He tried to sit up but she placed her hands on his shoulders "Don't try to get up …."

"My head hurts," he said simply, laying back on the pillow. "I've been having a bad dream too. I dreamed that you were dead. Why does my head hurt and why is it bandaged?"

"You fell and cut your head on a stone," she said, hoping it would be the right thing to say.

He seemed satisfied with the explanation but tried to sit up again. She restrained him. "The doctor said you'd have to stay in bed for a bit. You'll be up in a few days."

He looked at her a long time. "You used to rub my head when it hurt," he said accusingly, childishly.

She pulled her chair closer and began to massage that part of his head that was not bandaged. He sighed and relaxed, soothed by the methodical movements of her strong fingers. The touch of his skin under her hand made her chest ache and a tear collected in each eye, and her breath became labored. He smiled and caught her hands in his.

"I think if you'll kiss me, I can go to sleep now." His words stabbed her like a poniard ... she'd have to ... she couldn't even think it out ... hesitate ... nothing ... go through with it. She bent over him and kissed his lips with infinite tenderness His hand went behind her head pulling her close. When he let her go, he smiled and lay back on the pillow. "Don't stay up too late . . . ." He was asleep.

Geraldine sank back in the chair exhausted, her breast almost bursting from the charging emotions it housed. In the morning it would all be gone. For a few brief moments she had been loved dearly ... mistaken for some one who was dead. In the morning he would remember nothing ... nothing. In the morning he'd be the boss again and she'd be a colored maid who worked in the house. Geraldine bent forward and buried her face in her hands, weeping.

Toni backed suddenly away from the door, her eyes burning from a hot surge of tears. She had witnessed the entire tableau and had watched every emotion that passed over Geraldine's face. She felt suddenly ashamed that she had been watching and yet she was conscious of a curious exultance. She glanced at Lavender's door and smiled victoriously through her tears. "You haven't been a wife to him," she thought, "but in the end the laugh will be on you." With a long shuddering sigh, Toni turned and made her way back to her room.

CHAPTER NINE

T WO DAYS AFTER HE WAS SHOT, JEFF sat on his verandah with a tall glass of iced tea in his hand. Toni sat beside him and watched him from the corner of her eyes. He seemed wrestling with some problem. His brows would knit up from time to time and he'd gnaw pensively at his lips.

"Something on your mind, Pop?"

Jeff started guiltily. "Er ... no ... *yes!* I feel fine, the headache is gone, but do you know I had some strange things happen to me when I was cracked out from the bullet."

"Like what?"

He frowned again and stared for a while out across the lawn. "It's hard to tell just how it felt but I had the strangest feeling that I was with your mother." He grinned. "Maybe I died and we met again in spirit."

Toni did not join his attempt at lightness. "That could not have been," she said with deadly seriousness. "You were not hurt that bad."

"Oh, I know that," he said deprecatingly. "I was just kidding but it was the most graphic thing I ever had in a dream. It was plain as day and yet I ... ." He hesitated.

"What, Pop?"

He frowned again. "As plain as it was, there's a tiny feeling that it wasn't her at all. Oh, hell ... the whole thing is silly."

Toni said nothing but she could see that he was under tension by the little muscle that twitched like a tortured caterpillar at the corner of his mouth. He savaged the bit of his pipe and tried several times to light it.

"It was her and yet it wasn't her," he said half to himself.

"Could you explain that a little better, Pop?"

He shook his head. "No, I couldn't. I know how foolish it sounds but there it is. I saw her as plainly as I see you and yet I have an equally certain knowledge that it wasn't her."

"You probably had fever," she said. "People have strange dreams at times like that."

"Sure, sure. I know. I've had nightmares and dreams before, but nothing like this. It was entirely too plain for a dream and it was a pretty shoddy thing for fate to do, too." His lips closed hard and stiff over his pipestem. Toni turned her head so he wouldn't see the tears in her eyes. She blinked rapidly and caught them surreptitiously in her handkerchief as they emerged from her eyes.

"What did the sheriff have to say?"

He took his pipe from his mouth and smiled. "It's great to be a figure in the parish. Alex assured me that I'd be put to no inconvenience. I'll have to appear before the grand jury probably but it'll be just a form. Alex knows."

"Has an eye on the November elections, eh?"

"Right. I'll bet a dollar Jasper and the rest of that rabble won't be molested either. Their vote counts as much as the next one."

"Someone should talk to Feathers."

Jeff nodded. "Someone should, but who would you nominate for the job?"

"I'm sure I don't know. I don't think I'd be up to it."

"Exactly. I've done some thinking on the subject and as I see it the only one—now this might sound a trifle silly but think it over—the only one to make the appeal is Bull himself."

"Say," Toni sat bolt upright, "it doesn't sound silly at all. It makes good sense. If Bull could be persuaded to see it … I'll bet he could make a good one too, after having run through that mill."

"That's the way it seems to me. I'd die of mortification if I had to tell her and since neither her father and mother chooses to realize what's going on, then you may be sure that any appeal to them would be asking for a row. I can see their looks of affronted dignity right now but you are sure they're bound to know."

"Of course they know. They are like a lot of parents...shut both eyes and pretend it isn't so. Just like Philip Wylie said...that a lot of people are sleeping with a lot of others but we just go along pretending it's all a lie invented by the communists or someone."

"I'd like to know what the initiating element was in Feather's case."

"It'll probably never be known. There's a lot that isn't known about the malady."

Geraldine came silently out on the porch and Toni watched her carefully. Her face was set but her eyes caressed Jeff as she stopped before him. "Can I get you some more tea, Mr. Jeff?"

"No thanks, Geraldine. I've been wanting to thank you for helping Toni the night I got hurt. She's been telling me how much help you were."

"That's all right, Mr. Jeff. I'm glad I could help. You got hurt trying to help Bull. There aren't many white people who would have done it."

Jeff smiled. "Well, Bull is worth helping. I could say I did it because it would have cost me a lot of money if they would have lynched him."

Geraldine took the empty glass from his hands. "You could say that, Mr. Jeff, but you won't." She turned and disappeared in the house.

"I guess that'll hold you for a while," jibed Toni. "You self-effacing people."

"It always makes me uncomfortable," he complained, "... Geraldine's directness. It takes away one's defenses."

"Those things can be an awful drag sometimes."

He looked at her quickly, but her eyes were wandering. "Yes," he agreed, "I can see where they would."

Toni's smooth brow furrowed slightly. "You know, so much has happened lately but I've been wondering. I haven't seen Lemuel in some time."

"Probably sulking somewhere after the beating I gave him. I wonder if he told on Bull." A sudden rage struck him. "I'm glad I thought of that... that you reminded me, I mean. I got a few things to talk over with him."

"Not now," she protested. "You're not well and a bout of anger won't help any."

That night at supper, Lavender, who had been as quiet as a mouse since Toni, in a storm of rage, ordered her away from Jeff the night he was shot, cleared her throat several times then asked, "Jefferson, have you seen Lemuel lately? I haven't seen him for days."

"No, I haven't," said Jeff shortly, "and if I find out that he set that mob on Bull, he'll wish he had kept going."

Lavender stopped eating and sniffled into her napkin.

"You are not at all charitable, Jefferson. Lemuel is not a normal boy. He ...."

"If he isn't, then the place for him is at Jackson," he said viciously. His temper was none of the best at the present and he was not feeling at all charitable. "He chases the colored women and if it keeps up, that's where he will be put. I've had enough of him and his trouble making."

"That *woman*," she put a wealth of disgust and poison in the phrase. "She's the one who made the trouble. She's the one that should be put in Jackson."

"Probably," agreed Jeff, "but she is not my daughter and it isn't my place to put her there. At least she keeps her mouth shut and doesn't go around shrieking that she's been raped. Whatever she does, she does in as much secrecy as people like Lemuel will let her."

Lavender buried her face in her napkin and ran from the room.

"Now," said Toni balefully, "we can enjoy our supper."

The next morning after breakfast, Jeff wandered to the barn where the music of trace chains told of work animals being readied for the day's work.

Overhead came the whistling whoosh of a buzzard coming in on a bombing run at dizzy speed. He watched it out of sight beyond the lip of the bluff, then turned to Limm, the cattle wrangler.

"Limm, jump on your horse and run over there and see what those buzzards are after. Some old cow must have fallen over the bluff."

Limm, long and cadaverous, nodded and leaped on his unsaddled horse and cantered toward the bluff.

Jeff walked on to the barn where he stood making suggestions and giving orders until gradually the Negroes had gone to their respective fields riding their mules sideways.

Having a slight headache, he walked back toward the house. He heard a clatter of hooves and turned to see Limm riding hard across the pasture. He had a handful of the horse's mane and was leaning low over its neck slapping it under the belly with the reins at every jump. Now what, thought Jeff, as he stopped. Limm slid off the horse and almost fell.

"What's the matter with you?" asked Jeff with irritation. "You look like you've seen a ghost."

Limm passed a quivering hand over his face and gulped noisily. "I done seen wusser'n dat."

"What is it?"

Limm swallowed again and clenched his teeth to keep them from chattering. "Hh-h-hit's Mr. Lem."

Jeff cursed beneath his breath. "Where?"

"Oo-o-over dey…stuck up on dat…dat ole car body by dat big 'simmon tree…musta fell frum de bluff…blow flies…Lawd…Lawd…."

Jeff leaped on the horse "Get up behind me." Limm did as he was ordered and together they struck out toward the persimmon tree that stood on the edge of the bluff where the pasture joined the woods.

Jeff was not normally a squeamish man but the sight which met his eyes as he rode up to the old car body nearly threw him. Lemuel was impaled as neatly as an olive on a toothpick, the windshield support having entered his back in the mid-thoracic region and come out just below the sternum. The torrid summer weather had turned him black and he was swollen almost beyond recognition. His jaws were spread wide open, his tongue, black and distended, protruded between his teeth in a leering grimace. A shred of flesh torn off by the blunt metal shearing through his body had clung to the end of the support and dried curling like a drake's tail.

His body had bent to a horrible angle, the feet in the front seat and the head resting on the rusty motor; his back broken and skull flattened from the impact. Swarms of blue bottle flies covered the body, their gauzy wings seeming to fan the tearing stench out, making Jeff clench his teeth against nausea. In the trees surrounding the area black vultures gasped and coughed asthmatic opinions back and forth among themselves waiting till the men should leave so they could resume their feast. So far, they had managed to do little damage.

Jeff picked up a branch and hurled it at the nearest tree and the birds launched themselves heavily into the air scampering upward, into the sky. "I'd better stay here with him, Limm, in case those buzzards come back. You go back to the barn and get one of those old haystack tarps. Don't get a good one because it'll have to be burnt. Tell…no just bring the tarp back and tell no one. I'll have to call Preston Varden to come out. He's the only one who can do Lem any good, now."

Limm took a look at the body and shuddered. "I wouldn't tetch 'im rat now fer a cahload o' 'possums. Mr. Varden sho weks fer his money." Limm leaped on the horse and cantered off. Jeff watched him as he threaded the narrow trail to the top of the bluff, disappeared, he looked back at the mortal remains of Lemuel and tried to feel sorry for the man. How had he fallen? Jeff looked back to the lip of the bluff. It was not humanly possible for Lemuel to have fallen from the edge of the bluff and struck the old car. Some other than natural agency had done the job because Lemuel would have had to leap at least twelve feet outward in order to strike where he did. Could he have committed suicide...?

No, Jeff shook his head in answer to the question. Lemuel wasn't the type, to begin with, and no one with more brains than a grasshopper would leap from the bluff as a means of self-destruction. If it had not been for the old wreck of a car Lemuel *might* have been killed but more likely he would have only gotten badly broken up. No suicide. How then and why? Could he have been thrown or pushed? Pushed probably, but he would have struck the base of the bluff some fifteen feet from the bottom because it began to slope outwards at that point.

Thrown? Jeff shook his head. Lem was no giant but he weighed all of one hundred seventy pounds. Being short, he looked heavier but even so what man could have simply picked him up and tossed him over the bluff like a sack of hay? Jeff pondered, listening for Limm, hoping he'd hurry. The stench seemed to follow him where he went, pulling big drops of sweat from him and his breakfast seemed very restless.

With an effort, Jeff tried to concentrate. Who, in the entire parish was strong enough to pick a grown man up and throw him bodily over the edge? Bull Fallon! Bull Fallon could do it with a bigger man than Lem and who had a better reason than Bull for doing it? Jeff's eyes narrowed. It was no certainty but it sounded reasonable enough to send him into a frenzy of action. Like a goat he ran up the side of the bluff holding on to vines and myrtle bushes. Twenty feet from the bottom he looked down. Five or six feet below him was a bump of red clay which was just right for his purpose, being lined up with the car.

Jeff leaped out and down, landing rump first on the hard ground. It jarred him horribly, making his recent injury send jagged knives of pain through his brain. He continued to fall and almost did the job too well. Headed straight for the old car, he had to perform an acrobatic twist that would have done credit to a circus performer and getting his legs under him for a second, made a terrific leap outward, barely managing to clear the car. He got up, walked over to a young gum tree, leaned against it and breathed heavily, holding his palms tightly against the gripping pains in his head. Sweat poured down his face and a fresh burst of odor from the corpse turned his stomach over so suddenly that he had no time to get set and had to let his breakfast do what it would.

Feeling relieved, he broke the top from a small pine and proceeded to beat the red clay dust from his khakis then he walked back to the fly feast and looked over the trail he had made in the dirt and grass. Eight feet above the body of the car, the trail ended making it appear that Lem had fallen from above and struck the ground to bound up and strike the car which was the only way it could have happened had the man actually fallen. Satisfied, Jeff walked away and sat beneath a tree. He brought out pipe and pouch and began to fill the bowl of the much used briar.

By the time he had it going, he saw Limm come over the lip of the bluff with a mouldy tarpaulin across old Dapp's haunches. As Limm rode up, his eyes were showing that amount of white about the irises which indicate great fright.

"Now what?" asked Jeff, prepared for anything.

"De law ... at de house," gasped Limm. "Stopped me and axt me wheh you wuz...."

"Well, why didn't you tell him?"

Limm's jaw grew slack with amazement. Telling the law *anything* was something Limm viewed with considerable alarm even during normal times. With a corpse on their hands things were distinctly abnormal ... so Limm reasoned.

"You means you want him *hyer?*"

"Of course. We'll have to get him some time, so why not?"

Limm shook his head vehemently. "I don' b'lieve in having no truck wid de law notime."

Jeff took the tarp from the horse and with one hearty swing covered the body and most of the car. "Now trot right back to the house and try to lie out of whatever lie you told in the first place. Tell Alex to get down here right now, but don't tell another soul ... got that?"

"Yassuh."

"Okay. Get going."

Limm got, showing by his reluctance that he could get along very well without any truck with the law.

Twenty minutes later, Alex Touchstone, followed by Avery Garder, his number-one deputy, came to the edge of the bluff. "What you got down there, Jeff," called the sheriff.

"Something pretty ugly, Alex. Come on down and see for yourself. Turn down the bluff to your left and take that cattle path down when you hit the woods. You can make it all right."

It took them ten minutes to travel the path and as they came up, Avery put his hand over his nose. "You got a corpse. Don't nuthin' else in the world smell like that."

Jeff nodded and together they walked to the old wreck. Jeff whipped the tarp from the body and stood back.

"Arrragh," croaked Alex, backing hastily away holding his nose and fanning at the flies that had been aroused.

"Jesus," mumbled Avery, under his hand backing away also. "Who is it?"

"It's Lemuel, my brother-in-law."

Alex took out a big pocket handkerchief and held it over his florid nose. "How'd it happen, Jeff?"

Jeff shrugged. "You got me. We've missed him for the last couple of days and since I had to beat the hell out of him the other day, I didn't think it strange. He was an odd one, anyhow. Furtive and sort of creepy. Stayed drunk most of the time."

"You say him and you had trouble, Jeff?" asked Avery, raising his eyebrows.

"Yes."

"What about?"

"He was chasing one of the Negro women and one of my men didn't like it, especially when he tried to get him to play pimp."

Alex shook his head.

"Who, Jeff?"

"Bull Fallon."

"Uh oh…" Alex flushed at the memory of the dilemma in which the attempted lynching and its repercussions had placed him. "That's the one they tried to lynch, ain't it?"

Jeff nodded. "Yes, it is." He didn't care to go into the matter, and neither did Alex Touchstone, who proved it by letting that facet of it drop.

"I doubt," said Jeff, thinking he'd better get in a word now, "that Bull would have done it. He had too much else on his mind and I know for a fact that Lemuel was alive at supper the same night. The mob caught Bull in bed and when he heard them, he took out for the house. After he had been freed, he was too beat up to do anything."

Alex nodded, obviously glad to agree in order to stop the conversation. Avery began to circle the wrecked car, looking for evidence. He stopped by one rear fender and looked up. "What'd he do, fly?"

"Looks like it," agreed Jeff. "Unless he jumped or was thrown."

"He'd be damn fool to jump," said Avery. "He couldn'ta knowed he'd light on that there old buggy and if he didn't he wouldn'ta done nothin' but get broke up."

Jeff nodded but said nothing and Alex pulled a stem of green bull grass and chewed it absentmindedly. "Nobody throwed him either," averred Avery looking up again. "They'da had to chuck him a good ten feet out before he'da lit on …. Hey, look up there." Avery scrambled up the side of the bluff, taking the same course that Jeff had taken, climbing it the first time. Avery stopped opposite the little ledge and pointed. "That's where the body landed. You can see where it rolled on down and hit that there bump and bounced. That's why it hit the car … bounced there and left the ground and stuck that upright through his belly."

"Never mind all the details," growled the sheriff. "We can see where it went through. I guess that's what happened. Avery, you go back and get the coroner. He'll have to see him before he's moved."

Jeff said, "Would you mind telling Pres Varden to come out … better tell him what sort of shape the body's in so he'll come prepared."

Avery nodded and started to leave. He turned to the sheriff. "Looks like to me that's what happened. He either fell or was pushed off the bluff. He lit up there and bounced onto the car." He looked at Jeff. "You can bet he wasn't throwed, Mr. Jeff. Ain't nobody in the world coulda throwed a man that size that far out." Jeff nodded slowly as though reluctant to believe it, at the same time heaving a silent sigh of relief.

Alex walked away and finding himself a tree, sat and prepared to wait.

"Do your folks know about it, Jeff?"

"They know he's missing but they don't know that he's dead."

"You might as well go on and tell 'em. I'll wait here till Avery gets back.... You go ahead and I'll take care of everything here."

"That's nice of you, Alex."

Alex jumped to his feet. "Not at all," he said heartily in his best campaign manner. "You go ahead and let me earn my money for a change.... Oh, by the way, I came out to tell you that you'll have to appear before a grand jury just so they find a no true bill and make everything right. Nothing but a form."

"Thanks, Alex," Jeff turned away. He was moved to vote for Alex not because he was a good man but because the ones running against him would probably be worse. Alex wasn't the sort to ruin his chances at the polls, and as a peace officer, he was good enough as long as things went well. Other politicians with a great deal more at stake acted no differently than he, so why hold that against the man.

When Jeff reached the house, he saw Lavender and Toni standing on the porch looking his way. It was a little too much to suppose that they had not suspected something to be amiss, what with all the odd activity, but he wished there was some way out of having to talk about it.

Lavender, he knew, would throw a fit and he didn't feel up to enduring one of them. His head ached and he was still nauseated. He felt he could still smell the stench and had an overpowering desire to take a bath.

Before he reached the steps, Lavender started. "What on earth is going on, Jefferson? Limm wouldn't talk except for whispers to the sheriff and...."

"You'd better brace yourself, Lavender."

Her hand went to her throat. "Oh...not...Lemuel?"

He nodded. He felt that if he had to be sympathetic, he'd vomit again, realizing suddenly how much in his life was gesture at which his instinct rebelled and how brutally he had beaten it down to conform.

Lavender swayed and leaned against a column for support, then she stiffened. "Tell me...."

Jeff mounted the steps and sank into a chair, noting as he did so a queer gleam of triumphant malice in Toni's eyes. Wondering passively at this phenomenon, he said, "He was either pushed, jumped, or fell over the bluff. He was killed instantly."

Now she'll faint, he told himself, and I'll have to catch her, but she didn't. Instead she sighed sadly and dropped her hands. "Poor boy," she said. "Too bad he had to come to such an end. He was a brilliant boy at one time."

Jeff sat up in surprise. "Lemuel?"

She nodded slowly. "Yes. When he was going to the University of Connecticut. He had a wonderful future... brilliant marks...."

"What happened?"

She turned on him like a tigress. "None of your goddam business," she screamed, her face distorted and burning with hatred and malice. For a few seconds she faced him, her eyes wild and flaming, then she turned and fled through the door into the hall and up the stairs.

"Well," said Toni, letting her breath go gustily. "What do you make of that?"

Jeff tried to quiet the leaping nerve in his face with a hard hand and shook his head. "You got me there, Kitten. She sure blew up didn't she?"

Toni sat beside him on the arm of the chair. "Why don't you go to bed, Pop. You're not well enough for all this. It'll make you sick again."

He rubbed his face. "Kitten, get on the phone and call Alcide. Tell him to come over here if he can possibly make it. I feel the need of a good talking to."

She got up quickly. "That's just what you need."

Jeff watched her slim curved figure disappear into the hallway and sighed. Everything was topsy turvy at Fomalhaut. A woman who had placed one of his Negroes at the mercy of a mob, then had rescued him. A daughter who had been raped in her own bed. A wife who was no wife at all. A brother-in-law who wanted Negro women but who was now dead. His own dream that was so graphic but untrue. The devastation wrought by Geraldine every time she was in his presence…

Dr. Fontenot was not in and couldn't be reached but Maud promised Toni she'd have him call as soon as he could be contacted.

"I'm going to have a cup of coffee, Pop. Care to join me?"

He nodded slowly. "Yes…I'll have one…anything to be doing something."

Toni left the verandah and sneaking into her father's room took two capsules from a box on his bed table.

Downstairs again she found Geraldine. "In about five minutes," she instructed, "will you bring a couple of cups of coffee to the porch and empty these two capsules into this deep blue cup. That'll be for Pop. I'll take the yellow one. It's that sedative Dr. Fontenot left. He's got to calm down or something'll happen."

Geraldine's eyes were softly understanding. "Yes, Miss Toni. I'll be there after a while. You go on back."

Toni walked back to the porch, feeling relieved. "Geraldine'll be here in a minute with the coffee, Pop," she said as she sat down. "Why don't you lie down for a while, after you drink your coffee?"

He sighed. "I'll try it if you say so, but I doubt that I could lie down and stay there very long."

Geraldine gave coffee to Toni first, so there'd be no possibility of a mistake and Toni, who had envisioned putting the cup near his hand so he'd take it, silently applauded the colored girl's cleverness. Jeff drank his coffee without gusto but with a certain grim determination. Fifteen minutes later he began to feel quieter and half an hour later felt a little drowsy.

"You know I might be able to sleep a little."

"Go to bed, Pop. I'll take care of everything."

"Nothing to take care of, Kitten. I've sent for Varden already. He'll remove the corpse after the coroner has taken a look. I guess they'll bring men out for the inquest. Tell 'em I can't be disturbed. Tell 'em I'm a sick man."

"Don't you worry," she said grimly. "They won't bother you."

CHAPTER TEN

A MONTH AFTER LEMUEL'S BURIAL, Lavender left for Connecticut to visit relatives and Toni and Jeff on orders from Dr. Fontenot left for a trip to the West Indies.

Lavender returned and finding them still away, promptly left again. In mid-September, Jeff and Toni returned and three weeks later, Lavender, for the second time.

Toni and Jeff were darkly tanned and looking very fit, as did the young man they brought back with them. When he was introduced to Dr. Fontenot, the doctor felt a quick twinge of interest because it was obvious that his presence made Toni ill at ease. It was also obvious that he was badly smitten with her, following her every move with his eyes and hanging on her every word.

Albert Fontenot walked into his father's study-surgery-office one afternoon and flopped in a handy chair. "Guess who I saw catching the plane at Harding Field this morning?"

"I'm not at all good at guessing games as you should know by now," said the father acidly, putting down his reel and oil can. "Who was it?"

"Tall, broad, and bronzesome... Toni's new fellow. Devall's his name, isn't it?"

The old man cast a malignant eye at his drink which melting ice had weakened beyond repair. "I glean from that hodgepodge of words that it was Toni's fellow you saw board the plane?"

"That's right and he didn't look happy. I tried to engage him in conversation and got an unintelligible mumble. All, I take it, is not well with the romance."

"Ummm … well, I'm glad you told me. I think I'll be paying them a visit." He put his reel away and put on a battered felt hat.

Jeff met the doctor at the steps with outstretched hand. "You must have heard my mental radar signal."

"Why? Something wrong?"

"Everything's wrong. Toni blew her top last night and I had to give her some of those pills you left me when I got that crease. She hasn't left her room all day and I can think of no good reason to go in. In fact I'm afraid to."

"I'll go up. A doctor has a ticket to every room."

In thirty minutes he was back, his face grave and still. He sat down heavily. "I had hoped for a lot from that trip. Too much maybe. She's right back where she was in the summer. We haven't gained an inch."

Jeff paled. "Is it that bad?"

"It's that bad. Devall stood it as long as he could then he seized her and kissed her … forcibly, the idiot."

Jeff brutalized the stem of his pipe. "I thought something like that had happened but I didn't dare ask. Just how bad do you think it is, Alcide?"

"It couldn't be any worse," he said without animation. "It's terrible. If I thought it would do any good, I'd recommend Askins. He's in Bainsville and the best psychiatrist I know and he'd come here but I don't think it would do any good."

Jeff shook his head slowly. "Well, that's that. If I had been able to do anything I'd say I've now given up, but I never did anything. I'm beat."

They were silent for a long time, each submerged in thought. Finally the doctor said, "Had any more raids by Feathers?"

"No, not a one. I made Bull go talk to her. It was a job and he was frightened to death but he managed it some way. He says that she didn't answer him yea or nay but I do know she hasn't been on the place since that night. Maybe she has other outlets."

"Let's hope so. Nothing ever came out about Lemuel's push or fall."

"There are two people ... no three that know the truth of it," said Jeff in a low voice. "Bull, Hilda, and me. He told me but I had about figured it out ... considered it at least. Lemuel attacked Hilda when she went for help. Bull had passed out from his beating, and Lemuel was about to succeed when Bull came to and heard the sounds of the fight. He came on the scene just in time, picked Lemuel up like a three weeks' old puppy and threw him over the edge of the bluff. He didn't realize at the time what he had done and it was not till Lemuel's body was found that he knew. They kept it to themselves till just before we went on the trip. It was the night before they married that they came to me and told me."

Fontenot smiled and tugged at his beard. "And you told them to keep their mouths shut."

"I did just that," said Jeff challengingly.

"I'm glad to know that," said a voice behind them. They turned to see the spare figure of Lavender standing in the doorway. They had been so interested in their conversation they hadn't heard her approach. She gave them a scathing look and disappeared into the house.

Jeff gripped his face hard with both hands. "Last spring it began to rain on this plantation. It has poured ever since. I wonder, Alcide, just how much a man can stand."

Dr. Fontenot's goatee bobbed up and down rapidly. "It is at times like this that I consider murder to be a very salutary solution. Don't let that remark make you do anything foolish, Jeff. If you kill her off be sure to burn the body and scatter the ashes. I'll say I took her to the train on the first leg of a twenty-year trip around the world."

Jeff grinned a little. "I doubt that I'd have the nerve to murder anyone, now, Alcide."

The doctor took his leave a little while later and Jeff sat in the gathering darkness staring out across the quiet lawn, his mind as much of a void as he could make it. When Lavender hurried past him wrapped in a short coat against the gathering chill, it didn't occur to him to ask her where she was going at this odd hour, until ten minutes later. Toni came quietly through the door and sat on the glider.

"Feel better, Kitten?"

"A little. Where was Lavender going?"

"I don't know. What say we slink off to town and see a Tarzan picture? I need some diversion."

"Why not?" She went into the house and got a coat, bringing him a leather jacket. "It's getting cold nights."

It was Limm Washington, complaining loudly and bitterly that everything happened to him, who found Lavender the next morning. Trembling and ashenfaced, he told Jeff about it. Immediately, even before calling the sheriff, Jeff called the doctor and they arrived almost together. Again, Alex Touchstone and Avery Garder went over the same ground, finding not a single clue. Dr. Fontenot, pleading age and infirmity, stood on the edge of the bluff and looked down … when he wasn't looking about. Then he sat down very suddenly, eased something into his pocket, then stood up immediately, unnoticed by anyone below.

Two hours later, the coroner's jury, remembering a similar "accident" was more cagey but scarcely more helpful in rendering a verdict of "death at the hands of person or persons unknown."

Toni, Jeff and the doctor were seated on the verandah. "I feel numb and stupid like I had been on a bender," said Jeff mechanically. "I didn't do it, Alcide."

"Hah," the doctor snorted. "I knew that. In your recent state of mind you wouldn't have done such an excellent job. Any prime suspects?"

"None, not a single one. I'm not up to any keen thinking lately, anyway."

"Why not me as a suspect?" asked Toni. "I can't think when I've ever been so pleased over anything."

Jeff smiled weakly. "Mainly because you were with me at a moving picture at the time of her death as guessed by the coroner and we both saw her leave the house as did Geraldine."

Something clicked in the doctor's mind and he closed his eyes quickly to avoid letting the light through. He felt the steady pressure of a hard object in his pants' pocket. He rose to go. "I'll have to be moving, folks. I'll be back tomorrow... going to have services here, Jeff?"

"No, I'm shipping the body back to Connecticut. I'm sending Lem's along at the same time. Nice gesture, you know. He wouldn't like to be down here all alone."

The doctor's eyes twinkled. "Indubitably... indubitably. I'll see you soon then... probably before the end of the week."

When the doctor arrived home, he routed Albert out of a textbook where he was looking up some strange malady. "I'd make him eat that book, Jane," snapped the old man. "Reading up on something that a soda mint will cure."

"He either reads or sleeps, Dad. There's nothing I can do about it. He claims I keep him awake a lot so he has to catch naps."

"He'd claim that as a defensive measure. Come on offspring. I have work for you to do."

Albert groaned and put his book down. "I like Cecil better than I do you."

"Never mind your impertinence... come on."

In the little laboratory back of the office, the old man took an object from his pocket and handed it to Albert. "Take a look."

Albert did. "What is it?"

"Dummy, it's the heel of a shoe."

"Am I to turn cobbler after a day's work as belly seamstress?"

"No, tell me what that heel walked around in. I'll be in the office having a drink with my lovely daughter-in-law. I hope it takes you all night."

Thirty minutes later, Albert called his father. When he entered the laboratory, his son wore a look of tired triumph. "There you are, my dear Holmes." He held out a sheet of paper on which he had jotted his findings.

His father scanned it. "Hummmm ... traces of food particles, namely protein, starch, vegetable matter. Saponified matter ... in plain English, soap. Well, it would appear that the heel had been in a kitchen. Scrubbing same probably. Wouldn't you say that?"

Albert nodded. "I'd say that. From these clues, I'd say the murderer is a famous chef who put too much red pepper in the chili thereby murdering the victim who had a passion for chili."

"And," said the doctor tartly, "if you did, I'd say you are the ass I have long suspected you to be. Now, Merlin, take that heel and that sheet of paper, plus your memory of the last forty-five minutes and burn them very thoroughly in that little furnace there. I do not ever wish to hear the subject mentioned again either in jest or otherwise."

Albert folded his hands in front of him and bowed respectfully. "It shall be done, my father, even as you say."

"You're dang tootin' it'll be done," said the little man taking a pull at his drink.

It was one of those sweltering September days that can at times outdo August. The sky was an inverted brass bowl that seemed to reflect the burnished disc of the sun and concentrate it all to earth. Not a breath of air stirred. Cattle, horses, chickens and man had sought the shade and relief, each in his own way. Trees were beginning to turn faintly yellow, brown and red, but as yet only the pecan trees and sycamores had lost an appreciable amount of leaves. It hadn't rained in a month and a fine coating of gritty dust covered all low growing vegetation.

Toni was in the lowest mood of her life. The future looked as black as had the recent past. She could still feel the quaking revulsion that had covered her when Phil Devall confronted her suddenly in the dark hall and kissed her again and again. She grew nauseated at the thought and sucked on a piece of ice which she fished from her coke. Phil was a fine man with a good future. He was clean-cut and handsome and in every way desirable and eligible. With Phil went her last hope of shoving into the mists of the past her revulsion at the touch of a man. She thought of Lemuel and Lavender. At least they were past all feeling. If they did not enjoy or thrill to life, at least they did not harbor hopelessness and despair.

Drawn by an almost hypnotic desire to see the spot of the other two deaths she dropped her house jacket to the floor at her feet and donned shorts and a halter. There was an automatic numbness to her movements, like a sleep walker.

She stood on the edge of the bluff and looked at the old car that had been Lemuel's death. Lavender, they said had been unlucky. If she hadn't broken her neck, she would have hardly been scratched. Unlucky... how did they know that? Had anyone ever come back to tell a story? She recalled a Jack London story about a coolie that was to be beheaded and the jailer tried to comfort him by saying the guillotine might even tickle.... no one knew just what it felt like. The coolie's last conscious thought had been that the jailer was wrong... it didn't tickle.

Maybe they were better off... maybe *she* would be better off. A shudder shook her but she took a step nearer the edge.

"That's the trouble with this country," said a voice. "No mountains. A little tumble like that would only sprain your ankle."

Toni gasped and whirled about. Sitting only thirty feet away, his feet hanging over the edge of the bluff was a young man. A man with humorous eyes that also had a certain look of cynical wisdom. His face was a little too craggy to be handsome but it was a good face with a very sensitive, slightly curved nose. His mouth betrayed his eyes because it was mobile, wide and she could tell it laughed easily and it had a certain tender quirk at the corners.

"Two people died on this spot," she said a little nettled.

"Wrong," he corrected easily and pointed. "Down there, and they were just unlucky…or lucky, depending on the point of view."

"I had no intention of jumping," she said, anger making her voice slip a little at the corners.

He shrugged. "I didn't say you did. You were considering it in the abstract, let us say. I'm sure that you were not standing at the site of two deaths wondering what you'd wear to South of the Border tonight."

"I don't think I like you," she said angrily for lack of something better.

"You haven't had a chance to think on the matter at all. I'd advise against any hasty opinions. It is much easier to defer than to change them."

"Oh, you know everything, don't you?" she cried, stamping her foot.

"Practically," he said with infuriating coolness. "I will admit that women have me stumped. The more I learn the less I believe."

"Now, isn't that just too bad? The womanhood of the nation should go into mourning."

"If I should die, there'd be a wave of suicides that'd make the country weep from one end to the other."

"Oh…" Toni was totally without words this time. He got to his feet and approached her, grinning like an adolescent. "Let's cut out all this nonsense, Toni. I'm Ike Blumendahl."

He held out his hand and for some reason, which she half resented, her anger drained out of her leaving her feeling very young and foolish. She took the hand almost shyly and they both burst out laughing. It was such a relief to laugh, that Toni went in over her head and she couldn't stop. Tears came to her eyes and she started crying. He caught her by the shoulders and shook her, but she only laughed and cried the harder. Regretfully, he released her left shoulder and slapped her a stinging blow on the cheek. She gasped, touched the spot and started crying, just crying. He drew her to his chest and smoothed her soft tousled hair and said kind things to her.

"There now," he said, as her crying slackened. "Take hanky and blow nose." She giggled shakily and blew loudly on his handkerchief, folding it neatly and sanitarily and handing it back to him.

"Feel better?"

"Much better, thanks. You ... you woman beater!"

"The old cave man stuff gets 'em every time. Nothing like it."

"Won't you come to the house? I'll build you a drink or something."

"I'll take the drink. I'm just out of school and I'm an inveterate gong kicker."

Geraldine served them the drinks on the verandah and as Toni arranged herself comfortably on the glider, Ike took swift inventory. Her legs were long and slender, but he could tell that they were not the soft spongy legs of the sedentary woman. They were hard and tan and muscular, straight and made to walk and run with. Her waist, where the halter exposed it, was smooth and narrow and he noticed the fine luminous quality of her skin. Her breasts were full, erect and excitingly pointed beneath their covering which all but failed at its task. He let a little silent quake of a laugh shake him from within. His mother had put this thing up to him as a task, which due to her unwise boasting had to be done to save the family honor. He could see that it would probably be the most delightful task he had ever undertaken. He recalled his paternal caresses while she was crying and decided that her revulsion wasn't as deeply rooted as was supposed. Her hysterics, the slap, plus confusion and anger had been stronger than the revulsion. He also sensed an unutterable relief, like the breaking of a long tension. Her face was placid and relaxed and her eyes were laughing and full of mischief.

"I guess," she said, stroking the moisture from the glass, "that I was pretty much of a baby."

"Men and women," he said, frowning at her, "have long placed the therapeutic value of tears second to a certain stupid loyalty to a calm exterior. The straight face under all stresses. There are things more foolish but offhand, I can't think of any."

She looked at him with wide eyes. "You know, you sound just like Dr. Fontenot."

"Then," he said, his eyes twinkling with good humor, "your Dr. Fontenot must be a very wise man. My mother said he's a devil that reads people's minds."

Toni sat up suddenly. "Oh ... you must be Missy Blumendahl's son. I didn't know she had any children."

"She had one. That one took all the time she had to spare."

"I'm ... I'm amazed. What on earth were you doing on the bluff?"

"Two things. I was looking at the river ... the view is superb and I was hoping you'd come out."

"Why, that's silly. Why didn't you come to the house? I'd have been glad to show you the view."

He shook his head vigorously. "Uh uh, I like it my way. I like to do strange things at unexpected times. Like for instance, as soon as I finish this drink, I'm going home and bathe and dress. I'm coming back to supper and then we're going to South of the Border for some dancing and possibly get a little tiddily."

She made a face at him. "How do you know I'll go with you?"

"I didn't ask, did I? There's just one thing. You mustn't expect any necking. I detest it and I never saw the girl I'd kiss." He didn't look at her but the angle of his vision showed the look of relief that passed over her face.

"I think I'll be able to bear up," she said with a chuckle.

"See there, you've agreed to go already. No trouble for the great Ike. Technique is what does it."

"I could refuse, just to burst that egotistical bubble."

"Then it would show that you were doing it out of vindictiveness which is a sop for small souls. I have every reason to believe that the dimensions of yours are positively cyclopean."

Toni burst into a gurgle of mirth. "You are the most abandoned nut I ever met."

He bent her an arch look. "Careful, squirrel. I have a thin shell but the meat is excellent. See you about five thirty."

He leaped from the porch and was gone. Ten minutes later she heard a car start just within the fringe of woods bordering the bluff. She sighed and laughed aloud. It felt good to be able to do that. She got up and went inside singing at the top of her voice. She was young, much too young to interrupt a happy mood with analytical thought.

As Ike escorted Toni to the car, he glanced appreciatively at the white dress she wore. He paid a great deal of attention to the exquisite fit and the delightful slide of her thighs beneath its softly draping folds.

"What do you call that material?"

"What? Oh … the material. I don't know. It's some sort of synthetic stuff I got in St. Thomas. A native woman made it and I don't think I ever had a dress that fit better."

"It is certain," he said with laughter just beneath the surface of his voice, "that a dress never had a better torso to fit."

Toni laughed easily, and felt a little surprised. Laughter hadn't been easy this past summer.

At the club they found an excellent colored orchestra and after the first round of drinks and a few games of bingo, at which Ike won a gigantic doll and fifty dollars, they took to the almost deserted dance floor. Toni was light as a feather on her feet, yet she was weighty enough to make Ike know he had an armful of delightful woman. Ike was tall and lithe and together they made people notice them. They both had perfect time and a flair for the exotic and spectacular. Ike bribed a rhumba from the band with Toni's recent trip in mind and they wriggled swiftly into the first steps. Toni suddenly tore away and walked quickly to the table. Ike followed, his eyes narrowed, not in question, but in intense concentration. As she sat down, they opened ... he understood.

"I'm sorry, Ike, I ... ."

He waved a hand to indicate that it was nothing. "Never mind, squirrel. I was sort of weary, anyhow. Waiter?"

"Yassuh."

"Another round of drinks, only this time, make them double." The waiter nodded respectfully. He moved away.

"Who'd expect to find a nice place like this way out in the country? I heard about it from some tourists up in Maryland and I made a mighty vow to visit it."

"Does it equal your expectations?" she asked reluctantly following his lead.

"Surpassed 'em. I'm a clubber by nature. My mother was one before me."

Toni felt a warm rush of affection for Ike. The little unpleasantness he had ignored so totally that it might not have happened. She wondered what had turned him against necking.

"How does it happen that you are so averse to necking," she said in a bantering tone.

"You won't change my mind on that. It ain't sanitary."

"A bacteriophobe, I take it?"

"Dyed in the wool."

"Well, I wasn't about to twist your arm. I just wondered about it. Unusual to say the least."

"You have known me only a short time," said Ike with a grin. "Just wait a while. You haven't scratched the surface."

"I'll bet I haven't."

"You will allow me to hang around, won't you?"

Her face darkened. "I'm sort of contaminated, Ike. Maybe you hadn't better."

He was silent for a moment and when in curiosity, she finally mustered up enough courage to look, he had a grin on his face that showed what a sound set of sparkling white teeth he had.

"Is it that funny?" she said, sparking a little.

"It's twice that funny." He sobered. "What made you pick me for such a thorough-going dunce as to be moved by any mass reaction? I know all about it. My mother has an espionage system that'd make the F.B.I. look like Junior Red Ryders. She knows everything and she doesn't misvalue much." He stopped and looked at her seriously. "What say we whip this goddam thing, Toni?"

The waiter brought the drinks and Toni seized hers avidly and tossed it down. She tried to see Ike again but tears made him an indistinct blur.

"No one can help me," she said through tight suffering lips.

"That's right," agreed Ike. "*You've* got to do it. All I can do is to try to keep you occupied, kid you along, and come around once in a while, since it seems that the manhood of this country is such that you're lucky to find out about it so soon. Think what it would be like married to one of them."

Toni reached over and seized Ike's drink.

"*Put it down, Toni!*" His voice lashed her across the face like a whip and she almost dropped the drink in her haste to obey the blazing command. Ike, then smiled at her so winsomely that she weakened, the rage died like a guttering flame and she held her face in her hands and wept from sheer nervous relief.

"That's the ticket, squirrel. Snort and slobber to your heart's content, then we'll blow hard and dance."

Her head came up and she wiped her eyes. "I could *kill* you."

"Faith and bejasus, and whoi would ye be after murtherin' me, now?"

"Because you make me so mad I could scream and before I can even open my mouth, you've done some silly thing to make me all…."

"It's that weird mixture of Hebrew and Deutsch…a sort of composite magnetism which mows down all opposition. We can't have you funnelling drinks and getting topply. Not here. Some night we'll go out on Big Buff Creek and get stinko but you're in the public eye right now. That's all they'd want, you know. You'd not only be a loose woman but a loose drunken woman. I'm sorry I barked at you but you are so fast with the flagon."

Toni clenched her hands and her eyes supplicated. "Promise you won't ever hate me."

"That's a promise. You couldn't make me hate you. I can be a pretty hateful person at times…. Let's dance."

CHAPTER ELEVEN

MISSY BLUMENDAHL CROSSED HER thick legs, shut one eye and gazed at the sunset through her glass of Bradsher's Special Age. "And so you feel that Alcide's pessimism is unwarranted?"

Ike Blumendahl shoved his hands deep into his pockets and after much searching brought forth a battered lighter with which he proceeded to set a cigarette afire. "Didn't say that. I said that things are not impossible. From necessity, Dr. Fontenot had to view the situation from the angle of a retired but entirely capable practitioner. He couldn't be expected to effect the sort of transference that I could."

Missy shoved a cigarette into one end of her long mellowed ivory holder. "What do you know about transference, you impertinent pup, and you not dry behind the ears yet?"

Ike eyed his mother severely. "Madame, I shall have to require that you speak of my father's most outstanding son in a manner befitting his station. Did you think it took me all that time just to finish medical school and my internship? You are speaking to a most brilliant psychiartist."

"Cats and dogs," moaned Missy, "and here I expected you to make a name for yourself in the South with your wonderful practice and you turn out to be one of those things."

"My dear and revered mother, how much money have we?"

"Plenty," said Missy easily. "Don't let that bother you."

"It doesn't. I might point out, though, that there aren't enough good psychiatrists in Louisiana to play a set of tennis doubles and I'm intending to supply a long-felt need. I'm to be the much sought after consultant. I'll lend my services at certain times on certain special cases. Say a couple of days a week at Jackson, a day in New Orleans every now and then, one in Baton Rouge, and all that sort of delightfully slothful rot."

"You're no son of your father's, if you can be slothful."

"I think," said Ike putting down his glass and lighting a cigarette, "that an inquiry about supper is the most harmless thing I can think of right now. What are we having?"

"Chicken pie a la Mandy, green salad, steamed cauliflower with Roquefort sauce, rice and gravy and blackberry cobbler with thick cream."

Ike let the breath steam from him slowly. "Ahhhhh ... let's to the festive board, Mater. I have worked up an appetite."

Some time later Ike moved away from the table a few inches.

"I shall have to invent an entirely new term. To call this a meal is leaving so much unsaid. Look what's left over."

"It won't be when Lula, Mandy and Louis get through with it. By the way when does your next treatment of Toni come up?"

"Tomorrow. We will agalloping go over hill and dale and in some cool spot we shall dismount, pluck violets and sniff geraniums. In short, we shall commune with nature."

"Better leave your personal natures out of it. She isn't that much improved is she?"

"Unfortunately, no. Even the rhumba is too fundamental for her tastes at the present but strides are being made. Last night she almost licked my hands when I let her little act of revulsion go unnoticed and regaled her with my inimitable brand of chatter."

"Suppose you fall in love with her?"

"Well ... suppose I do? It's a fairly common phenomenon and I must say it holds no fears for me. She's just my type and never in all my searching have I located a more breathtaking collection of structural divinity. She is a bit of all right."

"Right overhead," said Missy reminiscently, "in my room I saw something once that I never thought I'd see. I made a girl disrobe and take off her underthings because her wedding dress wouldn't fit them. It had been cut to fit her and it refused to accept her lingerie. Her body was the most utterly beautiful thing I have ever seen. It just wasn't real."

"Oh, yes, that big Fourth of July wedding you had that time. You wrote a book-length letter about it. I wished at the time that I could have been here. She must have been a dream."

Missy nodded. "She was and that's about all one can say."

As Ike prepared for bed that night after having been warned again by Missy that the servants' quarters were out of bounds, he heard a light tap on the door.

"Come in."

Lula came into the room, her usually bright face dulled with thick embarrassed blood. Her eyes strayed to the floor in front of her and stayed there. "You want some hot tea or sumpn', Mr. Ike, befo' you goes to bed?"

"Er … no thank you, Lula." He let a glance crawl over her a little slower than he had previously and more completely. She had changed to a simple well-fitting blue dress which was cut low at the neck, revealing a delightful crease which began high and disappeared downward. "I don't believe I want any tea."

"Yes, sir." She turned reluctantly to go and threw a glance over her shoulder.

"Er … Lula." She stopped and faced about.

"Yes, sir."

"Where is your room?"

"It's de fust one you comes to on de left of de hall." Her eagerness was manifest.

"Who else stays down there?"

"Mandy sleeps 'cross de hall frum me."

"Mandy's sort of nosy, isn't she?"

"Yes, sir."

Ike, his eyes lit with a devilish light stood up and walked over to where she stood. Leaning over he whispered in her ear.

She giggled and nodded vigorously and, turning about, left the room.

Ike showered and donned a soft silk robe. Walking to the window he looked out on the broad moon-splashed lawn where sheep and cattle grazed quietly. He tied his robe loosely at the middle and lit a cigarette, tossing the match out on the verandah just outside the window. It rattled softly on the old cypress flooring. Ike listened to the raucous clamor of the silence and smiled. He had only been to this place a few times but he loved it with a passion that he found hard to explain. He wondered how city people ever got so accustomed to their brawling smelly existence that they could prefer it to the peace and sweet cleanliness of the country, where the air was fresh and you had room to move about. He had been reared in New York and had hated it with gusto ever snice he could remember. When he graduated from high school Missy had moved back to the old place and Ike visited her at intervals. Now he was here to stay and ....

He heard the door creak open and since the light had been turned off he waited for some signal. He heard a low whisper calling his name. He turned around and walked across the room seeing only the dim shadow of a woman by the door. He came up to her and touched her shoulder. It was bare and still damp from her bath. Its fine texture sent an electric shock up his arm. He reached up and slipped her robe off the other shoulder and with both hands stripped it down the back. He embraced her and felt the excitement that filled them both.

"Mr. Ike ... oooo ... Mr. Ike ...."

CHAPTER TWELVE

JEFFERSON SALTON SAT ON THE verandah and had three large drinks in rapid succession. Granny Rosa watched from the hallway and shook her head. Jeff tried hard to think but he couldn't. His body and mind demanded and his past revolted. It started a football game in his head and he squeezed it between his palms. The vision of Geraldine floated before his eyes and a tremendous ache came up in his chest. He saw the vision of Antoinette immediately following and cringed but to his surprise she did not seem angry. Then he remembered her last words before she died. "Don't grieve for me, Jeff. Live! Live as we have lived. Love life … love living." He had thought she was sleeping and she was … the long, long sleep. Tears came to his eyes and a hard sob jerked him from chest to knee. He drank again and again until his thoughts shrieked shrilly in a cave of resonant walls, their voices beating back and forth till his skull shuddered to the impact of a thousand impulses, orders, and the screeching voices grew louder and louder. He held his head hard and whimpered like a wounded animal, the sound bringing Geraldine out on the porch.

"Are you sick, Mr. Jeff?"

He raised his head. What was she doing out here … laughing at him when it was all her fault, all her fault? He leaped to his feet, swaying dangerously.

"Get out of this house," he yelled.

"But Mr. Jeff…" Tears came to her eyes, making Jeff sick with self-disgust. He took the refuge which has been the outlet for distracted men since the world began. He completely lost his temper.

"I said get out!" He swung his open hand which cracked sharply against her cheek. Geraldine didn't flinch, she didn't move. She just looked at him for a few seconds, then turned and walked slowly down the steps. Jeff attempted to make it to his room but only got as far as the sofa of the living room.

Dr. Fontenot found him there four hours later. He looked down at the prone figure and tugged angrily at his beard. "What happened, Granny?"

"He drunk too much."

"That's obvious, all right, but why did you call me?"

Granny sighed. "Come back in de kitchen and I'll fix you a cuppa cawffee."

Over coffee Granny told him all that had occured. "He hauled off and slapped her in de face. Dey wusn't nuthin' she could do but go."

"He was out of his mind," muttered the doctor grimly. "He's getting to be more of a problem than Toni."

"She young," opined Granny succinctly.

"That's right. Youth has a lot more bounce. How does Geraldine feel about it?"

"I don't know suh. If I know her she ain't gon' git on no high hoss."

"Sensible woman."

"She knows things, too," said Granny pulling fiercely on her pipe. "Mah ole man uster beat me onct er twict a mont'. I likened t' cut his throat wid a lamp globe onct, too. Us uster fight ever now'n den."

Dr. Fontenot smiled a little. "Is that the reason Geraldine doesn't mind?"

"Sho. I knowed mah ole man didn't mean t' be bad, and she knowed de boss wus drunk and all tore up in de head. Dat gal ain't no fool."

"Who's that talking back there?"

"Don't tell 'im I called you," whispered Granny. The doctor nodded and went back into the living room. "Well, you decided to wake up, huh?"

Jeff sat up and swayed. "Wow, what a head!"

"Granny, bring three aspirins and a cup of hot coffee," called Fontenot.

After three cups of coffee Jeff began to feel better. "Nearly dark outside. You haven't seen mine and Missy's offsprouts, have you?"

The doctor nodded. "Yep. When I passed the swimming hole coming out here they were apparently leaving the water. They'll be in in a moment."

"Mustn't let them see me like this."

"Right. I'm going to give you a pill and send you to bed. I hear you ran Geraldine off."

"Yes." Jeff's jaw hardened and his lips grew thin. "I couldn't stand to have her about."

"Was it necessary to slap her?"

"Give me the pill, Alcide. I'm in no condition to match wits with you."

"You never were," retorted the doctor. "Take this with a little water and hit the sack. I'll see you tomorrow on something important."

Jeff went upstairs to take a bath and tumble into bed. He was asleep almost instantly. Granny, seeing that he had left the light on tiptoed upstairs and turned it off. She stood watching him for a while then shaking her head she turned and waddled out closing the door softly behind her.

The next afternoon at four the doctor showed up again, his face serious and his step rapid and purposeful. "Good afternoon, Jeff," he said as he bounced up the steps. "You look a little shaky."

Jeff smiled ruefully. "I'm shaky as a groom on the way down the aisle. Have a chair and a drink."

"You been hitting it again?"

"No, just put it out for you."

"Why don't you have one?"

The other shuddered. "No thanks. I can't gauge it anymore."

"Then I'll gauge it for you." Dr. Fontenot poured. "There, now, dump that small one and in fifteen minutes I'll give you another."

Jeff drank and grimaced. "If I had that other one right now I think I could make it thirty minutes."

"Yes…probably." The doctor poured again and handed it to him.

"Now, let's get down to business and to start it off I'm going to tell you a story of some people I know because they remind me of you. The man of the family had a shrew of a wife who couldn't see a thing but social life and parties and ancestor worship and the like. Her husband couldn't see it at all but he let her go her way. This woman was an odd sort who seemed to have no sex response at all and before long they were sleeping separately. The man in confusion and frustration took to drink. After so long a time a servant came into the house who was quiet and dignified and … well, beautiful. She obviously loved the master and he found a strange attraction in her, but there was the wife, and there were his inhibitions engendered by years of white supremacy. It started a war within the man that threatened to upend him. Then one night his wife fell from a precipice and was killed … ."

"This story is a little *too* much like me." Jeff's face was gray and tense, the nerve leaping uncontrollably in the corner of his mouth.

"Shut up and don't interrupt. As I was saying, everyone thought the wife fell from the bluff but she didn't fall."

Jeff leaned forward, his hands clenched into steel hand balls. "What makes you say that?"

"Several things. First, the man had told a doctor friend of his a secret which his wife overheard and knowing his wife he had a strong suspicion that she'd make trouble. It is reasonable to suppose that others overheard also and knew that the wife had overheard and that she'd make trouble. Later that evening the wife left the house. The reason will probably never be known but she did leave. The next morning she was found dead just a few feet from where her brother had also been found impaled on a piece of steel on an old car body. The doctor friend went to look at the scene staying on the bluff and while there discovered a shoe heel which looked new. He took it home with him and analyzed it, finding that the wearer had been employed in a kitchen. It was not hard to test the heel and find that out. He burned the heel and up till today has never mentioned it to a soul and from this day on never will. He told it today to try to prevent the man from making any bigger ass of himself." The doctor sat back, his beard bobbing furiously, and quaffed his drink.

Jeff sat in his chair like someone who had been slugged with a sandbag. His hand wandered absently to his face and massaged the lean jaw. For a long time he looked sightlessly at the floor. "Looks like we won't have any rain before Christmas, Alcide. Things certainly are dry."

"That's right. I'm having to water my fall garden every afternoon and Maud is complaining about the quality of the beans. Here, Jeff, have a drink." The doctor poured him a stiff slug and handed it to him. He drank it gratefully and sighed with something like relief.

"You're the only doctor I know who prescribes whiskey for his dipso patients," said Jeff with a stiff grin.

"I'm the only doctor you know who knows which patients to prescribe drink for. I'm not afraid of your drinking, Jeff, once you get straightened out."

Jeff fell silent for a while, taking a little longer to down the last drink. He seemed to be able to think a little clearer, and the first sting of the shock was clearing away. "She did it for me," he half whispered.

Dr. Fontenot said nothing but drained his glass and refilled it. Out to the northeast of the house he could see Toni and Ike galloping across the broad pasture on their way to the Big Bluff Creek swimming hole. He nodded to himself and smiled as he watched their horses come close together and the mock fight that ensued. Ike pulled her from her horse then led the horse rapidly away forcing her to follow and beg. Fontenot could hear their laughter and shrill banter and felt a sense of complete comfort and well being. "Look yonder, Jeff," pointing a finger.

Jeff looked and nodded. "The boy'll have her straight in no time if he knows what he's doing."

"And I'll bet my hat he knows what he's doing. Cuss that Missy. I wanted to do this job myself but she had to horn in. She had the right sort of man available and I had married mine off a year ago to Allen Gordon's niece. I doubt that I could have done it alone."

Jeff got to his feet and walked to the edge of the porch. "Let's walk over by the bluff, Alcide."

The doctor nodded agreeably and leaped to his feet. Together they walked across the broad grassy meadow toward the river. In the distance an old stern wheeler fought upstream, white puffs coming from her exhaust stack. A spurt of steam squirted away from the whistle but it was minutes before the rasping hoot came to their ears. The grass was dry and dusty and as they walked along their shoes raised clouds of the powdered clay making their shoes pink. High overhead a flock of egrets winged along in perfect formation.

"It was right here," said the doctor pointing at the ground. "I saw it and sat down and slipped it in my pocket. I didn't say anything because I wanted to know more about it before I did. I'm glad now."

Jeff gnawed nervously at his pipe and nodded. "She did it for me," he said again his voice soft and wondering.

"And for herself…that is to say, Bull and Hilda. I dare say she ran quite some risk and maybe someone else saw something but after this long it would have come out if it was coming out."

"My God, I hope no one else saw her," said Jeff fervently. "That would be the last straw."

"When are you going to fall off your bluff, Jeff? You've been teetering around for some time. What is it going to take?"

Jeff massaged the back of his head like it was aching. "I don't know, Alcide…I don't know."

"She has loved you since she was sixteen, you know," said the doctor casually. "She has never had anything to do with another man."

Jeff stopped dead in his tracks and turned around. "Say that again."

The doctor obliged. "You should have known, you ass. She did everything but write it out."

A great light burst on Jeff and he understood clearly what his background had been trying to confuse for him. Everything had a steel etching clarity now. "Let's go back to the house, Alcide, I want another drink…if I can have one."

"Sure, have one…have two if you make them small."

All the way back to the house his step had a curious spring. "Things begin to look better, Alcide," he confided with a certain bubbling exultance. "About Toni, I mean, you know, coming along like she is."

"I know exactly what you mean," puffed the doctor almost trotting to keep up. "And what's all the hurry?"

Jeff grinned like a schoolboy and fell into a shorter stride and as they reached the verandah he dropped behind and grasping the doctor under the armpits tossed him easily to the porch. The old man squealed and beat at the hands as they released him. "Goddammit, turn…let…but hell you've done it now." He brushed off his clothes and adjusted his tie. "Sit down and calm yourself," complained the doctor, "and drink your drink. I take it that you have come to some monumental conclusion?"

Jeff downed his drink in a gulp. "Precisely, as you would say." He reached over and placed an affectionate hand on the older man's spare thigh. "Missy didn't have anything to do with this, Alcide. You did it all yourself. I'll never be able to thank you enough. You have been the saving of both Toni and me even though Missy might have supplied the means for Toni's deliverance."

"Oh, do shut up, Jefferson Salton and fix me a drink. You have unnerved me."

Dark came early as it was nearing winter. Dr. Fontenot refused the invitation to stay to supper and left.

Jeff lighted his pipe and sank back on the glider. He felt content yet he was taut and nervous. Must be that binge he went on yesterday, and yet he had had enough tonight to calm his nerves. He wasn't nervous exactly. It was. ... He decided he didn't know what it was. He bit down on his pipe stem and sighed. He hoped Geraldine wouldn't be too sore at him. He deserved it for striking her but he hadn't meant to. It was a sort of hysterical impulse that came on him before he could head it off. He finished his pipe and stoked it again. He didn't feel at all sleepy. Fontenot's pill, no doubt. Too much sleep last night.

Two pipes later he began to feel a slight chill in the air but he was so comfortable that he was reluctant to move. He saw something moving toward the house coming up the driveway. Whoever it was had on light colored clothing and he could see the figure long before it got to the porch. Thirty feet away he could see from the free and easy stride that it was Geraldine and his stomach knotted up and a freezing fear came upon him. Hastily he grabbed the whiskey bottle and took a terrific drink which seared him from gulp to gullet. She came slowly up the porch steps and stood before him. The moon was just coming up and he could make out her calm face in the dim glow.

"Hello, Geraldine … I … er … did Granny tell you what I said?"

"Yes, sir."

"Well, I'll repeat it. Yesterday I was miserable and confused and unhappy and drunk. I'm really sorry for what I said and for slapping you. I don't know why I did that."

"I think I know why, Mr. Jeff, but it doesn't matter." She stood there looking at him with her soft steady eyes which were making him decidedly uncomfortable.

"Come," he said in a strange voice. "Sit here a while."

She sat with her usual grace and lack of embarrassment and the small size of the glider made her quite close to him. She had evidently bathed recently and he could smell the lingering fragrance of her toilet soap. It was a good clean smell. The last drink of whiskey was making him feel exultant and transcendent. "It was good of you to come back, Geraldine, but you needn't have come till morning. That is … I mean, I'm glad you came but I …"

"Yes, sir. I know what you mean. I came because I wanted to, Mr. Jeff."

"You wanted to?"

"Yes, sir."

"Why?"

"Mr. Jeff, you don't know?"

Again that agonizing knot in his stomach, the feeling that he was about to break out in cold sweat. He sat back and relaxed, forced himself to relax. "Yes, Geraldine, I guess I do know."

"I knew you didn't mean anything when you slapped me. You were all upset and everything."

"I'm glad you feel that way. Some people wouldn't."

"I'm not some people, Mr. Jeff. I'm only Geraldine."

The moon came over the fang-topped pines and shone brightly on them, revealing Geraldine's tear-wet eyes but her face was still composed.

Jeff sat up with a start. "Why are you crying?"

"I don't know, sir. It looks like I've wanted to cry for so long. I don't think I can hold it back much longer."

Jeff was stung to the quick. "Was it as bad as that?" He didn't recognize his own voice.

"It's been bad but not till lately has it been almost more than I could stand."

She caught her face in her hands and her smooth shoulders heaved with deep sobs that hurt him every time they shook her. He placed his hand on the nearest shoulder.

"Geraldine ... I, what can I do? I haven't intended to hurt you ... I ...."

She straightened up and made a magnificent effort to control herself. She seized his hand in both of hers and looked at him through her tears. "I know that, Mr. Jeff. I know you haven't meant any of it but please, sir, have you ever been ... been ..." A shudder ran over her and her head drooped again.

"You mean in love, Geraldine?" His voice was gentle and full of understanding.

She looked at him gratefully through her tears. "Yes, sir ... For nine years and only *see* the person. Never able to speak a word ... that's what I mean. I guess I'll never be able to tell you, tell you that. No matter how much I ..."

Jeff's head began to reel. The poignancy of the situation was a knife deep in his vitals twisting, twisting .... Suddenly he could see Geraldine on the brink of the bluff looking over. Lavender had already taken the plunge. He could almost hear her say, "You wouldn't, so step aside and let one who can and will." He slid over very close to her and took her wet face in his hands.

"Geraldine, would it help if I said that I know just what you have gone through and that I know what you've done for me … us, Toni and I, and that I …."

She grabbed his arms in a grip so hard that it hurt. "Please, sir, don't say it … even if you mean it. Not now. I have hoped all these years that I could just be your woman. I know you better now. You wouldn't just take any woman. It means more to you than that. It does to me, too." She couldn't go on. She rested her forehead on his forearm and wept bitterly. Jeff was cut to the very depths, the drink was confusing his thoughts again, Geraldine's nearness making his blood course faster and faster. Then it struck him. His mind flashed back to the night of his dream. It was Antoinette and the conviction that it wasn't her at all. Now he knew. It had been Geraldine. Something in her nearness, her touch … something, made the light burst upon him with dazzling brilliance.

A strange calm came to Jeff and in some way her head came to rest on his shoulder. He put an arm about her and drew her close. She looked up wonderingly and as she did he kissed her, softly at first with respect and gentleness, then nature's demands, long dammed in both of them, broke and flooded. Minutes later they parted and looked with wonder and awe at each other. For a long time neither spoke, just looked.

Geraldine took a long shuddering sigh. "I've waited so long for that, Mr. Jeff … so long."

Jeff breathed deeply and his face took on a ruddy hue. "I guess I have, too." Then he backed away. "Geraldine, this … this thing isn't fair to you. You stand to gain nothing but …"

"That's all I want, Mr. Jeff. Don't think I haven't thought about it through and through a thousand times. It can't be any other way so that's the way it'll have to be. We can't make over the world so we'll have to beat it. We'll take what we can and get whatever happiness we can without their vows and rituals and their good will. I'll be the house girl and I'll be near you to serve you and see that you're comfortable. And at night, whenever you wish .... What more could a wife do except bear your children? I'll even do that if you want me to but I don't think it would be fair to them."

"Geraldine, you're an immensely intelligent person, a much better integrated person than I am."

She shook her head and smiled, showing ivory white teeth, even and regular.

When they parted this time they said no word but got up and started for the north side of the house. They found a stairway there and climbed it to the second-story verandah and entered Jeff's room.

An hour later the moon crept slantingly through a window and threw a golden saber across the bed. Jeff had not gone to sleep but she apparently had. Her face reposed in utter peace, her breath coming in the regular rhythm of perfect health. The beam of moonlight struck her across the stomach at a sharp angle and reached to her forehead, caressing the smoothly flowing rise toward her firm erect breasts, touching them and sending tent shaped shadows against the amber perfection of her skin.

He sighed and laid a caressing hand on her velvety expanse. Her eyes opened and she smiled softly.

"I thought you were asleep," he said half accusingly.

"Not asleep, just relaxing." She caught him in her arms and strained him to her with tender yet demanding pressure. His breath came sharply through his nostrils and they shifted. She cut short a sibilant gasp, his muscles tensed and a wave of shattering passion engulfed them.

Jeff waked the next morning with a sense of wellbeing that he hadn't felt for years. He glanced guiltily at the empty space beside him then smiled and relaxed. A tap came on the door and Geraldine entered. "Good morning, Mr. Jeff." Her face wore the same placid reposed look it always had. She put the tray with coffee, cream and sugar on the little bed table.

"Good morning, Geraldine, did you sleep well last night?"

Her smile sent dimples deep in her cheeks. "When I slept, I did very well."

He caught her arm and pulled her over on the bed.

"Be careful," she whispered. "Miss Toni is awake."

He held her close for a moment then let her go.

Geraldine gathered up the coffee utensils she needed and stood up. "I'll go now and take Miss Toni's coffee."

Jeff sat upright in bed. "Can you come again tonight?"

She didn't answer immediately but studied him intently for a moment. "Mr. Jeff, I'll come any time you say … any time."

He felt a knot in his throat and tried unsuccessfully to swallow it. "Yes," he said huskily, "I know you will."

She turned and left the room.

"Here," said Geraldine to Toni, "don't try to drink that lying down. You'll scald yourself." Her voice had an authoritative ring and she punctuated it by knotting up a pillow and placing it behind the girl's shoulders. Toni laughed inside. Geraldine sounded just like a mother and she remembered what Dr. Fontenot had said.

"Geraldine, this is very nice of you to bring me coffee. You haven't done it before."

Geraldine smoothed the girl's hair gently as she moved away. "I don't think I've ever felt toward you, Miss Toni, like I have the last few days."

"You've been acting very maternal and possessive," said Toni with a smile.

"That's the way…. *Oh, Miss Toni, please try to understand.*" Her eyes were aswim with tears of supplication.

Toni felt a sudden pain in her chest. This woman had feelings, emotions, fears, hopes and a heart. She suddenly felt proud of her position as she remembered what Dr. Fontenot had said, "It's a wonderful thing to be loved. Never question it." Toni's voice was low and vibrant. "Come and sit by me, Geraldine. There now. You love me because you love Pop … isn't that right?"

Geraldine nodded. "You know then?"

"Yes, Geraldine, I watched through the door that night when he thought you were mother. You've sort of felt that way ever since, haven't you?"

The other nodded, tears dripping from her eyes. "I can't help it. I'm just hoping you'll understand, not hold it against me, not hate me, not..."

"*Geraldine!*" It was a cry of pain, of pity, of gratitude and understanding. A cry that held all the loneliness of a spirit that had long been starved for the affection and gentleness of a mother and who at long last saw it in a woman of another race. They wept tears of relief on each other's shoulders and pride fell vanquished by another nobler and closer emotion, the need of one another in personal harmony.

CHAPTER THIRTEEN

MISSY BLEW INTO IKE'S ROOM THE next morning wrapped in only a few dozen yards of chiffon housecoat that billowed out behind her like a barrage balloon.

"Well…gad, look at that bed! Who slept there, a litter of pigs?"

Ike put down his coffee cup and looked saddened. "I am not a pig, Mater."

"You're worse than that. What gives at the Saltons?"

He shrugged. "You mean beyond her attachment to the way I spray words around…."

"You know what I mean, you bent-nosed mongrel."

"Please, Mater … my sensitive…."

"To hell with your sensitivities. You know what I mean—the way you met her, for instance. What was that for?"

'Multifold purposes," said Ike eyeing himself in the long mirrored door of the armoire. "People who meet formally must spend precious moments going through a ritual which is worse than that used by the Chinese because it is fatuous, purposeless and unlovely. It took Toni and me about forty-five seconds to become bosom buddies. My justly famous charm played quite a large part, I am reluctantly forced to admit."

"My, but I have a smart son! I know just how reluctant you are to admit it."

"What are we eating this morning?" he asked, switching the subject.

"Food," she barked and swept from the bedroom.

Ike lay on a colorful beach robe, his eyes closed against the fierce rays of the sun. By his side, on her stomach and elbows, making figures in the sand with a slim finger lay Toni. She was wearing a sky-blue bathing suit which gave the demoralizing impression that it had been painted on with a spray gun. For some time neither had spoken and the only sound was the lazy gurgle of Big Buff as it wound its slow way to the Mississippi, and the rurppp rurppp of the horses grazing on the bluff above them.

"Ike!"

"Yeah!"

"What are you thinking?"

"That question brands you as a female female."

"Double, huh?"

"Double with a vengeance. I'm quiet, therefore I'm thinking, therefore I might conceivably be thinking of you, therefore you want to know what it is. Plucking a phrase from the middle of that sentence upon which to comment, I might say that at this particular time, even though I have my eyes closed, if I were thinking of anyone but you I should be bled dry and my veins filled with vinegar and red pepper."

"That would embalm you."

"Yes, I could be eaten without seasoning. The pepper would lend piquancy and the vinegar would tenderize..."

"Oh, Ike, shut up. You make me ill."

"Very well, then entertain me with a fast commentary on man, morals and society."

"I'm afraid I couldn't do that very well."

"Why? You can talk, can't you? That's all that's necessary. If you spoke stupidly it's a lead pipe certainty that you wouldn't speak with nearly the amount of stupidity which characterizes ninety percent of the gabble on the subject."

"That's not much encouragement."

"I guess not. Yet I find that some of the less informed people speak very well about it if they have a fair amount of intelligence and some theological superstition hasn't amputated the part of their brain usually used for free thought. I had a very devout Baptist landlady once who had more sense per cubic centimeter of cranial space than any ten of the men she listened to every Sunday. She thought! Therefore, it was inevitable that she should come to some very sound skepticism. A great deal of it would have caused the elders to give her the old heave-ho had she spoken it about too freely. As is often the case she looked upon me as damned anyway so I was the recipient of many a long discussion. What she really wanted was some support on certain rather abrupt departures from doctrine. Naturally I gave her the desired support because she was a pretty keen-minded old lady and her idea had snap and aim."

"Ike, how good are you at projecting yourself away from your surroundings?"

"The best. Once I projected myself right out of jail where I had been incarcerated for pinching the deacon's bottle while prayer was in progress and getting pickled before the collection plate was passed. I dipped thereinto and …"

"Oh, Ike, be serious. I mean it."

Ike rolled over very close to her and his dark soft eyes looked squarely into hers. She felt their impact like a physical blow. These sudden transformations of his were disconcerting but this time she didn't avert her eyes or move. "Squirt, squirrel," he said smiling, taking some of the sting out of his abrupt act.

"What I mean is … you're a psychiatrist. What's wrong with me and how am I doing? I feel that I'm improving but the fear is still there. Will I ever lose it?"

Ike rolled over on his back and closed his eyes. "No spik English."

Toni sighed. "That's why I wanted you to take a distant and detached view of the thing and tell me. I knew you wouldn't do it if I didn't ... why won't you tell me?"

"Because, squirrel, there's no point to it. Naturally you are anxious to know and naturally I'd like to tell you but you must forget the psychiatric angle entirely. As you have seen, I'm not practicing on you."

"That's what I mean," she cried sitting up. "Why aren't you? You're here every day nearly and it looks like the opportunity would be too much for you to resist."

"Smatter, ain't my company enough?"

She was hurt and when she spoke she was near to tears. "I didn't mean that, Ike ... you know I didn't."

"I'm sorry, squirrel, but can't you just leave it as it is?"

She was silent so long that Ike opened his eyes and sat up. She was looking down the creek at nothing. "I'm going to say something and if it sounds silly then I'm sorry, but speaking in cold detached terms surely you must have thought that I might fall in love with you, pr you with me?"

"The eventuality has occurred to me, yes, as has marriage, a cottage with roses, vines and children. What's wrong with the picture?"

"You're deliberately making me draw a map," she said angrily. "Do you think that's quite fair? You must know that you're only making it hard for me."

"Squirrel, you're being thick."

"In what way, pray?"

"Well, let's take one of your possibilities. Suppose you fell in love with me?"

"Well?"

"Wouldn't that mean you were cured?"

Toni looked at him with miserable eyes. "I didn't know," she said finally, "that I was that thick."

Ike grinned engagingly. "You'll survive." He sobered instantly. "Let's you and me make a bargain."

"Like what?"

"Like this. Just let things go on as they are. Let me come over as often as I can. We'll play and fight and kid and in general disport ourselves as two adolescents should. We'll swim till it gets too cold. We'll ride and when fall gets here we'll hunt quail and go to see the L.S.U. football games and maybe to New Orleans to see Tulane when they have an especially good game. At any time during that period if I think you're cured I'll tell you so. Bargain?" He stuck out his square hand with its long sensitive fingers.

She nodded and gripped his hand. "Bargain, Ike. You're a very nice man."

" 'Fer sho,' as Mandy would say. How could you have ever doubted?"

She leaped to her feet. "Race you to the water."

He scrambled up and after a short chase caught her at the water's edge. He stuck out a foot and tripped her and she tumbled into the shallows. She sat up coughing. "That…was a d-d-dirty trick."

"Natch. I'm full of 'em. Wait till I pull your pigtails."

At South of the Border that night Toni was beautiful. The weather was still warm and she wore a light blue dress that was almost in two pieces. The short sleeved jacket reached the skirt in the back but the front showed an expanse of tan skin that made Ike's mouth water. Her hair had dried riding back to the house and she had brushed it till it shone like burnished gold. Her eyes sparkled and laughter bubbled easily to her lips. They ate all the pizza they could hold and after the proper waiting period had several drinks which made Toni's eyes sparkle all the more. Ike excused himself and went to the men's room and on the way back noted that Toni had taken similar refuge in the ladies' lounge. With a quick lunge he swerved and walked quickly to the bandstand.

Flipping a folded dollar bill to the big yellow Negro who led the band he said, "A rhumba, Jackson. The most savage and abandoned thing you can think of. Do it well and there'll be another buck coming up."

The Negro grinned, showing two rows of shining gold teeth. "Yassuh! She comin' up aftuh dissun us playin' rat now."

"Jackson, you're a positive jewel," said Ike elegantly. "I shall remember you in my will."

Ike arrived at the table some three minutes before Toni came back. He had ordered another round of drinks and was busy readying his glass for more.

"If I felt any better, Ikey," said Toni as she waltzed toward her seat, "I'd be ill."

"Maybe you will be before the night's over."

"Crepe hanger."

"Want to finish this dance, squirrel? The rhythm sends me."

She was on her feet almost before he finished speaking. "I feel especially lightfooted tonight."

"Mademoiselle," he said bowing low, "if you are any lighter than you have been previously I shall be forced to squeeze you mightily to hold you on the floor."

"Sir Ike," she said bowing in return, "your kind but flagrantly fallacious fabrications fill me to the full with gratitude."

"I shall have to remind you," grated Ike in her ear, as they moved smoothly across the floor, "that snappy speeches are my exclusive province and I shall resent any further intrusions... Damn!"

The music stopped and swung immediately into a slow primeval rhumba. The lights went dim and the walls and floor turned a dull red from the special lighting effects. He could feel the muscles in her smooth back go taut. Her lips compressed into a hard line. "Let's dance, Ike." Her words were as brittle as thin ice and her eyes were tight with determination.

Ike caught her by the arm and started back toward the table. "As I was saying, there is nothing so irritating as to be able to do some one thing well, not that I can't do innumerable things well; to do something well, then have that position usurped by a mere fluff of a female."

Toni was subdued and quiet when she sat down. Ike rattled on as though they had sat down only because they had tired of dancing. A slim, red-headed boy of about twenty-three detached himself from the crowd at the bar and came toward the table.

He had a clean, well-scrubbed face and a generally wholesome appearance. He was neatly dressed in a chocolate brown double breasted suit with brown and white shoes. A white handkerchief hung casually from his breast pocket.

"Hi, Tom," he greeted her as he came up to the table.

"Hello, Frank," she said without enthusiasm. "May I present Mr. Blumendahl, Mr. Holliday?"

Ike stood up and shook hands allowing that he was positively overjoyed to meet any friend of Toni's and managing to say it in a tone that made her throw him a quick glance. If Frank thought the greeting a shade too flossy he didn't show it.

"Haven't seen you lately, Toni. Where've you been keeping yourself?"

"The same place," she said coolly. "I don't move around much."

Frank was momentarily flustered and was more so a moment later.

"Why haven't you been out?" she asked.

Frank turned scarlet. "Well, you see we've been rounding up for the fall branding and ...."

"I meant during the summer. Unless my memory is playing tricks on me you were pretty well underfoot for some time. Then I didn't see you any more."

Ike kicked her under the table but she ignored him. Frank was suffering and looked about for rescue.

"I also recall you making the remark once, Frank, that what you did was your own business and Vanetta didn't have any control over your actions. Did she draw a gun on you?"

"You've got it all wrong, Toni. You see ... I ... that is ...."

"That's what I thought all along, Frank," she said smiling with acid sweetness. "Now you can run along. We have things to discuss."

Frank gulped twice and beat a hasty retreat. The back of his neck glowed like a tail light.

"That was just a shade unkind," said Ike mildly. "Are you going to suggest that I turn the other cheek? He happens to have been one of the most attentive and persistent of my swains till my little accident and from then till now I have neither seen him nor heard a word from him."

Ike's planed face grew hard and bleak. "One of these, eh? I didn't know."

"Furthermore, he came to me. I didn't go out of my way to be ugly but I'm afraid I'm not noble enough to put on a show now that Missy Blumendahl's son is seeing me, thereby making me socially okay."

Ike was pale with anger. "Is that true?"

"Oh, very. He and several of his cronies wouldn't miss one of her parties for anything. They are among the faithful who think that anything she does or even implies, as we have seen, is simply the voice from Olympus."

Ike rubbed the back of his head and blew out his breath with a gusty whoosh.

"I am a man of peace," he said with soft deadliness. "I think public brawling is both vulgar and ridiculous. However ...." He looked toward the bar, his eyes burning hotly. Suddenly he was on his feet, and before Toni could stop him he was several strides in the direction of the bar.

Toni started to her feet, arrested the motion, then decided to continue. With great deliberation she walked toward the bar.

Ike tapped Frank on the shoulder. "A word with you, my turkey-necked friend."

Frank turned around and proceeded to live up to Ike's description. "What is it?" he choked.

"Miss Salton asked you a question but you didn't answer it. Your pressing business has no doubt been taken care of by now and I'd like to hear what it is."

Frank as have many before him took refuge in anger because he was not equal to the question.

"What's it to you?"

Ike quirked an eyebrow amusedly. "You still haven't answered the question."

"Think you can make me?"

"I hadn't entertained the notion but now that you mention it . . . ." He slapped Frank so hard across the face that he almost went down. Immediately there was an uproar. Men backed away and Frank came back with a roundhouse that was tagged with stars but Ike stepped inside it, let it whistle harmlessly by his ear and dug his left into Frank's unprotected midriff with a curious hitch of his shoulder. An involuntary sound came from Frank's throat that was neither a cry nor a gasp, having qualities of both, generously decorated with bits of breakfast, dinner, supper, and whiskey. Ike stepped nimbly out of the way of the debris and backed a few feet away. Several strong-looking men came from nowhere.

"No trouble in here, buddy," said one, catching Ike by the arm.

Ike looked the fellow full in the eyes. "You will take your hand from me," he said softly. The man, having dealt with men some years of his life, stepped back without feeling that he had been abandoned by his courage. Toni touched the man on the arm. "There won't be any trouble, Jake."

Jake grinned. "Okay, if you say so, Miss Salton."

"Thanks, Jake. Ike, let's sit down."

Ike allowed himself to be led docilely back to the table.

"You were wonderful, Ike, and I'll have to admit that I very deliberately came to the bar to watch it well done."

He smiled and shrugged. "Frank's outdoor life has not hardened his stomach. It was as soft as the udder of a cow. Interesting collection of regurgitory jetsam. He evidently likes to put on the feed bag."

"Let's go home, Ike."

"After a decent interval," he said calmly lighting a cigarette. "I should not like to have it said that I struck a stout blow then took to my heels."

"That," she said grinning roguishly, "should indicate something."

He nodded. "A remnant of my little, little, complex. I'll never be free of it I suppose because there will always be people who think Jews won't fight, what happened in the Near East recently notwithstanding."

They had several more drinks and seeing no belligerent signs, left. The top of Ike's convertible was down and the moon flooded it with silver light as they rode slowly along, headed south. They both sat deep in the cushions, relaxed and comfortable. Ike had noticed that Toni sat near him when she entered the car, something she had been careful not to do on all other occasions when they rode together. Somehow their hands touched and Ike closed his long fingers over her soft cool ones. She didn't try to disengage them and he sensed a kind of watchful tautness in her. He held her hand for several miles then put his hand to his head where he proceeded to tousle his thick black hair.

"I'm that kind of a sensualist," he said, "who likes to have his head massaged. I go to sleep in the barber chair and lie down grunting when my back is scratched."

"Shall I scratch your back?" she asked with a chuckle.

"Not now ... can't lie down and grunt. Other times, other places. I shall issue a rain check."

The cool night air whipped softly about them, laden with scents of all sorts from the pungency of pine needles to the sere smell of dying leaves, and the ever present subtle perfume of ripening wild plum. Overhead the pines seemed to arch their lofty heads while gum and oak squatted majestically at their feet. A night bird, his jewelled eyes shining in the glare of the headlights, waited till the last moment before springing into graceful flight to avoid the car.

"What are you thinking, Ike?"

"Not again!"

"Whenever you're silent I seem to feel mighty grinding thoughts giving off rays like some invisible lamp or X-ray or something."

"With such an instrument I could study your skeleton perfection which I freely predict without any previous information is the equal in every way of what the eye can see."

She pinched him in the side. "There, I asked you a sensible question and you darted off at a tangent as you so often do."

"I have a mind that leaps about like a phrenetic kangaroo. Some of my thoughts are the distillate of nobility, others are the distillate of dark seething evility."

"Yap, yap, yap, how you do talk on and on like the rent and taxes."

"Pure chaff, my dear, to obscure what I was really thinking."

"Now you are mean and I insist on knowing."

"Well, you asked for it. I was thinking that I have been in the big cities all my life and, having the eye for lovely, desirable women, I have seen what I thought was the best. Yet, here I come into what I thought would be a rather backwoodsy place and I find a gal whom the best I've ever seen before can't touch with a ten-foot pole. It's not only amazing, it's uncanny."

Toni was silent a long time. He let her think without interruption, feeling that she needed the time. Finally she spoke. "Ike, that was very sweet."

"In just what way I fail to see. I spoke what I believe to be the truth. If I can be complimentary and tell the truth at the same time the effectiveness is doubled and I suffer no twinges of conscience."

"Do you ever feel twinges?"

Ike grinned and lighted a cigarette. "Rarely. I'm a man of no morals but I afford sustenance for several rockbound principles. The principles are necessary for my self-esteem, and to see that I wrong no person. Morals in a sense are hats hung on a rack from which they fall ever and anon upon the proper pretext."

They were silent for several more miles.

"What are you thinking, Toni?"

She started a little. "That gag is tired."

"I asked you a question, squirrel, or do you think it's cricket to ask then deny me the same privilege?"

"I'm ashamed to tell you what I was thinking."

"Then you pay me little credit. Don't you know you could tell me anything in this wide world and it would be perfectly all right?"

"Yes, I do feel that way. Well, to be frank I was thinking about what if you fell in love with me. It would be sort of terrible ... me like I am and all ..."

She could see the muscles knot in Ike's clean-cut jaw. "And I think," he said in a voice that was soft but trilling with feeling, "that it would probably be the most wonderful feeling in the world."

A pain tugged at her throat. "But, Ike, you know how I am ..." She was very close to tears.

"If I'm willing to consider it, knowing how you are, why are you yelling?" He was rough and a little loud.

"I'm not yelling," she said in a strange voice. "I wouldn't want to hurt you."

"If you didn't want to hurt me badly enough you wouldn't do it."

It took her some time to digest that and by the time she had, Ike stopped the car in front of the house. They sat still for a moment, Toni watching him and Ike looking our past the bluff.

"Good night, Toni."

He seemed distant and cool and Toni felt the reaching fingers of hurt, knowing that she had no reason for feeling as she did.

"Won't you come in for a while?" She sounded like a small child begging.

In one of his flashing transitions Ike whirled on her and smiled broadly, his white teeth gleaming in the moonlight. "Not tonight, squirrel. It's getting late and for some lousy reason my head is trying to act up on me. I'd better be getting home." He could see the flooding relief surge through her and felt light and happy deep inside. Her face brightened as he opened the car door.

"I always forget that you have twenty or so miles to go when you leave me. Good night, Ike."

"Good night, Toni."

"Ike!"

"Yes?"

"I had the most wonderful time. I really did."

"Thanks, squirrel." He reached over and squeezed her hand. "I'm glad you did because I did, too."

CHAPTER FOURTEEN

"WHERE'S IKE," ASKED JEFF CASUAlly one morning as they sat on the front verandah.

Toni compressed her lips. "He's been sick." She didn't add that it shouldn't have kept him from calling nor that he hadn't seemed too sick when she last saw him.

"I had about gotten used to him about the place," said Jeff gnawing the stem of his pipe. "Seems to be a very likable lad. He sure can talk up a storm."

"He can that," agreed Toni shortly, then she straightened up. A buckboard had just turned into the drive and the two red morgans pulling it broke into a mad racing run toward the house. They skirted the live oak directly in front of the house and were pulled to a sliding halt a few feet from the steps. "Whoa, you hard-mouthed bastards," roared Missy as she sawed them to a stop.

"If," declared Ike, brushing gravel and spots of debris from his clothes, "I ever get rooked into another ride like this I'm going to have my head examined by the most competent man in the business who, of course, is me and having already made the examination I know in advance what the verdict will be … dementia paralytica."

"Ah, hell … git outa the buggy and let's sample some of Jeff's bourbon. It'll beat that jabber of yours a mile." Missy leaped out of the buggy to be followed slowly by a protesting Ike.

"Did I but care to I could produce reams of documentary evidence to refute …."

"Hiya, Jeff," boomed Missy as she mounted the steps.

Jeff, gasping from laughter held out his hand to her. "Come on in, Missy. Geraldine will have the drinks out in no time. Where've you been keeping yourself?"

"This sissy offspring of mine has been having a noble dose of the trots and what with this and that he's been a problem, laying in bed all hours complaining that he is unto the death or some such maudlin moaning... say, you're looking up. Last time I saw you, you looked like hell."

Jeff glanced at Ike and Toni who had walked to the other end of the verandah.

"Things have changed here somewhat for the better. Toni has improved to a remarkable degree and I guess I have you to thank for that... indirectly, at least."

Missy dismissed it with a wave of her plump hand. "Don't waste it on me, Jeff. I get a bang out of it. Now, what has happened to you?"

Jeff flushed and looked away. "What makes you think something has happened to me?"

"Oh, for Christ's sake, don't get coy with me... well, I'm glad to hear it. It makes a difference, doesn't it?"

It was an effort for him to face her but he made it and even managed to be bold about it. "Yes, it does," he said challengingly. "I had no idea how much difference it would make. Love, Missy, crosses many rivers and barriers."

She nodded vigorously. "I oughta know. I tried it twice and both times people said I was a fool because one was a Dago and the other was a Jew. I must say that I haven't a single word to utter about them except the best. They were as fine a pair of men as ever was. Of course, I had my troubles with them. Tony was sucked out of his stride by any skirt that passed and Ike thought about business too much but I'm glad to say that I dealt with each in my own way and everything turned out all right."

At the end of the verandah Toni leaned back against the corner column and faced Ike. Her dress was of green gabardine and it fitted with that breathtaking exactitude which is calculated to produce disturbing emotions. Ike was properly impressed, eyed her boldly and noted that she took it in stride. "Allow me to say, squirrel, that you present a picture which for sheer feminine elegance has no peer."

She curtsied and her face shone with pleasure. "I never tire of such talk. Tell me more."

He noticed that she had unconsciously drawn her shoulders back and her stomach slightly in which resulted in her breasts sprouting upward against their restraint. The effect was dizzying.

"Sorry I didn't get over the last few days. I ..." He stopped on the verge of telling a lie.

"Yes, I've wondered why. You didn't seem too sick when I saw you last."

Ike clamped his lips shut in a tight line and mustered his courage. "I wasn't sick."

Her eyes opened a little wider. "Then ...." She stopped not knowing what else to say.

An inspiration struck Ike then which almost blinded him. That was the answer and although it was no less dangerous it at least gave what he might use as a valid excuse.

"Let's go for a ride. I can't talk here and I've got to talk. Can we use your car?"

"Of course. It's around the side of the house."

They got in the convertible and drove off. Toni whipped the car suddenly from the road and plunged into the woods on what seemed to be little but a trail winding between the trees. They rode along through the fall woods with its brilliant leaves and baring branches for a mile, then stopped in a little natural clearing, showing that they had made a half circle and come to the bluff again.

"This used to be a favorite smooching place," she said lightly as she braked the car to a stop. She spun on the seat and faced him. "What's the trouble, Ike?"

He deliberately allowed some time to pass before speaking. "Toni, this association is getting the best of me."

"I was afraid of that. I could see it, so what now?"

He shook his head. "I don't know. To tell you the truth I don't want to fall in love."

"But why? You said ...."

"I know what I said," he retorted roughly. "I just said too much I guess." He propped his jaw in his left hand and looked at the bottom of the car.

She slipped over near him and took his hand away. "Ike, look at me."

He looked and the sight cut him so deeply that he felt a physical pain. If ever there had been a portrait of love painted on a face Toni was now that canvas. It was aglow, surpassingly lovely in spite of its strong cast, her eyes wells of tenderness and desire. Ike took her in his arms and drew her close, sliding past her parted supplicating lips, buried his face in her soft fragrant hair. For a time he held her then as he drew away he miscalculated and her damp warm mouth encompassed his. For the space of a moment he felt as though some blunt instrument had slugged him a mighty blow back of the head and his senses spun, darted, and floundered crazily. Then with a mighty effort of will he tore away and sprang from the car. "I never neck," he said in a foreign voice.

"Ike, tell me what's wrong." Her voice was deep with feeling which held an agonized note.

"Nothing's wrong. I'm afraid I'll fall in love with you and I can't, that's all."

"What would be so bad about it?"

"You'll just have to take my word for it. I can't explain it." He came to the driver's side and got in, making her move over. Then they drove home in total silence.

Toni and Jeff stood on the porch and watched the flashing departure of Missy's team.

"I don't understand Ike at all," said Toni in a sobbing voice. Jeff looked at her but couldn't think of anything to say.

"Er ... Alcide called up. Wanted to know how you were."

Toni gave a startled exclamation and leaped into the hallway where the phone was.

Dr. Fontenot helped Toni from the car. "Come in, my dear. I called because I was afraid of something like that and I wanted you to have someone to talk to if you wished."

"But I don't understand him at all, doctor," she said very close to tears as they walked up the strip of concrete from the street to the house.

In the office he helped her into a chair and sat down opposite her. "Now, tell me what happened."

She told him everything. "And all of a sudden when I ... well, I guess it crystallized when I saw that he was holding back. Something came up in me stronger than any emotion I ever had. I knew I was going to kill that reticence. A woman only has herself to accomplish that with and before I knew it I was in his arms ... the old feeling gone and a bright new possessive feeling like the old me in its place. I knew then that I had whipped it, that I was a woman reacting like a woman should and I don't suppose I ever kissed a man like I did him. It simply laid him out, doctor, I know it did. I can't have been wrong about that. For a short moment Ike loved me with all his heart and soul then he tore away and I couldn't get through his defenses again. We went home then and I'm about crazy. What *can* be the matter? Do you suppose it has something to do with what he told me about never caressing women? He said that the first night I went out with him and at the time I was glad but later on I thought he must have been kidding me because in every other way he seemed normal. He said it again this afternoon."

Dr. Fontenot pulled at his beard and gazed at the ceiling. "Just sit here a while my dear. I must make a phone call."

He came back in ten minutes and his face looked pleased. A half smile toyed with the corners of his mouth. "Toni, I ... er, that is, *we* have a plan."

The sun went down on Fahenstock that afternoon in a sea of blood. A mighty roiling fire blazed and tumbled about the horizon in a perfect frenzy of extravagant color. Ike looked at it and caught his breath. "If ever man could reproduce something like that then I'd believe in art. As it is his puerile scrabblings have to be 'explained' in his own esoteric and abstruse terminology all mounting to a lot of pooh bah."

Missy sat, her glass on the concrete floor, and said, "I'm glad to know you can talk. You've been a perfect bear ever since we came back from Fomalhaut. Of course I'm sure Toni Salton had nothing ...."

"Then you advertise the total imperfection of your knowledge," he assured her testily. "She had everything to do with it."

"The honesty of the younger generation never ceases to be a marvel to me," said Missy crossing her legs with panting difficulty. "I was certain you'd give me an argument about it."

"I'd then have been a fool," he snapped, "and I've already come too near to it to suit me."

"In what way?"

"I almost succeeded in falling in love with Toni. At least I succeeded in curing her and making her think that I am in a sense as badly off now as she. I made her think I couldn't abide the amorous clutch."

Missy barked out a short laugh. "Any woman who has enough sense to spit out an olive stone would know what a stupendous lie that is. Ike, you are probably the world's best liar as was your father but the moment you step out of character you become the worst. Any announcement from you that the touch of a beautiful woman revolts you would have the ring of a lead coin on a glass counter. You may be the world's best psychiatrist since Strecker but you'd better listen to your mater on this."

Ike eyed his mother in morose silence. "You think it fell flat?"

"You kissed her, didn't you?"

"No, she kissed me."

"And you sat there like a log and didn't return it, I suppose?"

Ike looked a little crestfallen. "Any time I get kissed by a woman like Toni and sit there like a Sphinx and take it unmoved then I'm going to order thirty gallons of testosterone and drink it all at one sitting."

"Okay, then you spavined maverick, you think she didn't know that? Where'n hell are your brains?"

"Then it appears that I did make an ass out of myself?"

"You have been an ass for years," said his mother brutally. "Just my maternal affection has kept me from telling you."

Ike rubbed a day's growth of chin whiskers. "You sound as if you meant that."

"I do," she barked. "You're just like your father. You are brilliant but you have spells of thinking you're God. Neither of you ever recognized anything as being too tough to tackle."

Ike sat back in the big cane-bottomed rocker and pressed his fingertips to his forehead. For a long time he sat and thought, the only interruptions being Missy's strong teeth crunching ice, a habit which irritated him to shrieks. The more he thought the more confused he became, and all of a sudden the thought struck him that if he persisted in his attitude he'd likely lose Toni and the pain thus induced was sickening. He pictured her flying across a pasture on her big gray gelding, blond hair flying in luscious disarray, her flashing smile, the ready friendliness of her handshake and the wholesomeness of her comradeship. He pictured her long glorious body with the skintight blue bathing suit slipping through the water with the ineffable grace of a naiad.

"Mother, I'm miserable," he said in a rather small boyish voice.

It stung her with a quick deep pain and her big heart was filled to bursting but she fought the feeling down. "Well," she said with a lightness that surprised her, "when engaged in making a bed the possibility of having to occupy said couch should always be considered. You going to be at the party tonight?"

"Oh, for … no! Not just plain vanilla no, but *hell* no!"

"I'd like you to be. It will be a diversion and you'll meet some odd characters."

Ike considered. Anything was better than sitting alone in his bedroom all alone with his thoughts. "Oh … maybe you're right. Shall I dress?"

"By all means. Remember that this is the house parliament for society in these parts, and I'm the Queen Empress."

Ike attended the party and tried to get drunk to escape females ranging in age from twenty to grandma, all seemingly intent on the same thing, but something had happened to his inebriative quotient. He continued to drink but seemed to achieve no success at getting drunk so he lost his temper and with a wink at Lula went up the stairs to bed. She followed after a decent interval and remained an indecent one considering where she went.

The next morning Dr. Fontenot called Missy on the phone. "What happened?"

"Nothing," she fumed. "He drank like a fish, stayed upright as a Billikin, got propositioned half a dozen times and I more than suspect he went off with Lula."

"I compliment his taste," said Dr. Fontenot raffishly.

"Nuts. We're just going to have to try something else. Getting him drunk and working on him that way will first have to wait till he gets drunk and it seems that he never does. Is Toni there?"

"Yes," he said cautiously, looking back quickly to see if anyone was listening.

"Okay, then, just hold on for a while. He's out on the verandah pacing up and down like a caged lion and it's ten to one it'll work tonight. I'll call you if it does."

"What happened last night?"

"I made him attend a party and he ran into some girl who needed attention, medical attention, I think it was. He's been obscure about it. I intended for him to get drunk and he didn't."

"Very well ... do the best you can." Dr. Fontenot thoughtfully hung up the phone and returned to the living room where Jane and Toni were playing gin rummy. They quit as he came in and answered their questioning looks with a shrug. "Still no soap."

Toni bit her lips and her eyes filled with tears. "It's no use. After all, he certainly didn't come into this thing with the idea that he'd be snapped up into ...."

"You stop that," barked the doctor, his eyes sparking. "You must stand by and give the plan a fair trial. If you don't fight for your man then you don't deserve him."

Another night passed and still no word from Missy. About ten o'clock in the morning Dr. Fontenot answered the phone. "Alcide, I give up," came her strident voice.

"Give up? Have you lost your mind?"

"I'm well on the way," she said wearily. "I can't even get him to talk any more. He drinks but stays as sober as a judge. He paces the floor and has a vacant look in his eyes. He says he's not sure he's fit to marry anyone. I didn't mention anything. He offered that right out of a clear sky."

Dr. Fontenot's brow knitted in thought. "And what do you suppose he meant by that?"

"I'm sure I don't know but I do know I'm beat."

"Very well. I don't suppose there's anything ... ahh-h-h—"

"What?"

"I don't know yet but I just had a flash of inspiration. I'll call you when I get it straight in my mind."

The sun was two hours high and though it was shining bright the atmosphere had a definite chill. The grass had been touched with frost the night before, leaving the edges brown. Leaves cascaded from pecan and gum trees in a brown yellow flood, the breeze catching them and stringing them out over the meadow like an army in frantic retreat.

Ike Blumendahl sat on the verandah gripping the arms of his chair. He had been doing this for some time and finally the ache of his forearms filtered through his chaotic mind and he relaxed. Instantly his thoughts lined up in some semblance of order and charged down on him with a shock that brought him upright and gasping in his chair. Point one … you're losing Toni. His weak rebuttal that he hadn't wanted her anyway was stormed under in a twinkling. Point two … what if she does become really suicidal and? … that left his brow beaded with sweat. Point three … why did you go into this thing if you're going to let it wind up on this note? I didn't know it was going to wind up on … Didn't you, then why not? You're supposed to be clever and consider all the possibilities. You started off with a bang and now you've fouled up like a stumbling amateur. And while you're turning it over in your mind think this over: *Why are you sitting here in your own house battling yourself like a man sentenced to the death chair?*

A sob of relief escaped him as he saw Dr. Fontenot's battered little coupe turn the last curve approaching the house. Ike bounded to his feet and went to meet the little man.

"Allah be praised … am I glad to see you!"

Fontenot stepped slowly from his car, his face set and etched in lines of pain. "Maybe you won't be when you hear what I have to say."

Ike stopped dead in his tracks. The breath froze in his nostrils and a cruel icy hand clutched his throat. "What … ."

"I had a call from Jeff a few minutes ago ... half an hour probably. Toni has disappeared and she left a note that Jeff couldn't read to me so it must have been terrible."

Ike swayed in his tracks and every moment in his association with Toni flashed before his eyes like a speed mad movie. "She ... they didn't find her around the house?"

"Not a sign."

Ike passed a trembling hand over his eyes. A groan of sheer agony forced its way through his pallid lips. "Not in the house. Not in the...." His head came up in a flash. *Not in the house.* He wheeled about and sprinted around the near corner of the house. Seconds later his big convertible roared around the other side of the house like a runaway train. It made the first turn by the verandah and skidded madly, throwing gravel thirty feet out across the lawn. He yelled something at the doctor who stood slump shouldered, the picture of grief and dejection where Ike had left him. All he could understand of the shouted sentence was "... the bluff..." and Ike disappeared in a cloud of dust.

"If you weren't so blasted old," yelled Missy coming out on the porch, a drink in each hand, "the loss of Barrymore might be remedied. You can straighten up and come on in and toast your victory."

Grinning satanically the old man walked rapidly up the steps and accepted the highball from Missy. "You see," he said with amused spitefulness, "you couldn't quite bring it off without the delightfully delicate touch of the Great Fontenot. Oh, well, I shall be charitable. You did a fairly good job yourself."

Missy eyed him sourly. "Thank you, you gloating Franco-American bastard. Your charity astounds me."

When Ike skidded to a stop in front of the Fomalhaut plantation house he leaped from the car and shouted but not a sound could he hear in return. "All out hunting, I suppose," and broke for the edge of the bluff in a mad run. He reached it and stopped, his heart pounding his ears with audible blows.

Wheeling he raced along the rim for several hundred yards traversing the whole distance back of the house. He came to a fence and clambering over ran until brush and vines began to impede his progress. He looked swiftly about. No one could have gone through this without leaving some signs and there appeared to be none. He turned about, raced back to the fence and clambered over. Back in the pasture he made better time and soon came to the woods. He dove headlong into the wooded area, carefully keeping to the rim of the bluff, ran as swiftly as he could, stopping momentarily to peer over the edge cringing, each time expecting to see the girl's body at the bottom. Then he stopped short. Why wouldn't this same thing have occurred to the other searchers?

Ike felt somewhat foolish so he slowed down but did not abandon his search. Then he saw her. She was standing out on a little promontory made by the roots of a hickory tree that had held on despite torrential rains and wind storms. She was leaning against the tree looking out at the river three miles away across the flats. A wave of relief passed over him and he felt like crying. His stomach lurched and for a moment he felt as though he would be ill. His hands trembled violently as he dashed the sweat away. He must not frighten her—he'd have to be very casual and matter of fact about.... She turned and saw him.

"Oh, Ike, you've come back!"

She rushed to him and he took her in his arms cursing her in a low voice vibrant with emotion and relief. "Goddammit, Toni, what do you mean scaring the hell out of people, running off this way...."

She buried her face in the curve of his neck. "Nothing mattered, you don't love me ... Oh, Ike, why couldn't you have stayed away a few minutes longer ...."

He shoved her back and looked into her eyes. "All right, so I'm a heel. It took me a long time and something like this to make me see. I'm not a very good choice for a husband, either."

"Why, Ike?" Her eyes were damp but humor lurked in their depths.

"Because I'm just a natural pushover for women. I don't have any backbone where a skirt is concerned."

"Is that supposed to set you apart?"

"No, that is, I suppose a lot.... No! I'm not hiding behind the masses of males who seem to be like me or I like them."

She kissed him and he immediately proved his weakness by promptly forgetting what he was talking about.

Realizing what her kiss had done, Toni pressed her advantage, kissing him again and holding him tightly. This time she felt the dam break and knew that he was hers when his arms tightened about her in a grip of steel. Their lips mingled in passionate longing and as they lost consciousness of all else besides themselves, they fell to the ground together, still holding to each other. The deaths that had come about at this spot had wrought great changes in many lives; but what was happening here now had greater and more earth-shaking consequences....

Missy Blumendahl, Jeff Salton and Dr. Fontenot sat in the big living room at Fomalhaut and watched the flames of the fire dancing up the chimney. The weather had turned suddenly too chilly for the verandah to be comfortable.

"Well, Alcide," said Missy in a surprisingly mild voice, "we dood it again."

The little man nodded, sipped his drink and fumbled for a cheroot. "God bless youth," he said fervently, "even if they do cause us oldsters to outdo ourselves once in a while. I was beginning to think that Ike would prove too tough for us."

"That was something of an inspiration you had, Alcide," said Jeff laughing. "I'll never forget the look on the boy's face when he raced up to the house and called out. We were watching through the windows. For a moment I thought he had taken the wrong direction but he turned back. He came in so fast that Toni was almost caught in the house. She had just gotten to the woods when he jumped from the car."

The doctor puffed contentedly on his cheroot while Missy fitted a cigarette in her long holder.

"I think, Missy," he said, "that we'd better make a pact to operate jointly from now on. It appears that however we do it we eventually have to join forces."

She nodded somewhat suspiciously. "I make no commitments although the idea has its points. Whatever gave you the idea that Ike'd think about the bluff?"

Fontenot shrugged. "Ike's young but he's smart as hell. When I said she was nowhere around the house then I knew he'd think about the bluff. He thinks she was considering the leap the first day he met her."

Geraldine came in and replenished drinks around. She moved silently and obsequiously and left when she had accomplished the task.

Missy glanced at Jeff as did Dr. Fontenot, then they glanced at each other and back to Jeff who by this time was a healthy tomato red. A storm of laughter arose and Jeff said, "That's right, go ahead and laugh but I can always point to the shoves I got from you." He lit his pipe and puffed out a cloud of fragrant smoke. "And by the way ... thanks a lot."

Dr. Fontenot waved a hand and wiped his eyes. "Nothing but the best for a friend," he said. "By the way, Missy, the McKammon girl came back yesterday."

"McKammon ... who's she?"

"The girl Ike sent to Albert. She had an operation in New Orleans and it looks like a cure."

Missy nodded her head. "I'm glad," she said softly. "Now, if he could work the same thing on Feathers?"

"Bull would be glad," put in Jeff. "She hasn't bothered him any since she almost got him lynched but he's afraid she'll break loose again."

Missy sighed comfortably. "Looks like we're sort of gathering a nucleus, Alcide, from which to operate. You, me, Albert, Ike. Let's say we're the brains ... no reflections, Jeff." Jeff nodded and smiled.

"Then, let's say that we can count on Jeff, Toni, Allen Gordon, and Bonnie. Hank and Honey if they're not too taken up with their twins will be a good pair to help. Oh, yes, I think this gathering could whip almost anything we cared to."

"Please count on me in anything this side of murder to help any unfortunate person you run on, Missy," said Jeff earnestly. "If it hadn't been for you and Alcide I shudder to think what would have happened to us. As it is ...."

"This is undoubtedly the most delicious food I have ever tasted," said Toni.

"For which the Ming House is justly famed," mumbled Ike through a mouthful of fried rice and candied oxtail. "We are on the first leg of a trip which I confidently predict will draw gasps from you of all sorts. Here you gasp with delight as you will in Tutuila, Samoa, when you eat pig, fish, and chicken that have slowly been steamed in the earth for eight hours with yams, onions and red pepper. The pineapples are big as nail kegs and the bananas—you've never tasted anything like 'em. Papayas as big as street lights for breakfast and mangoes that taste like peaches that grew on cedar trees. You'll see!"

She smiled, her eyes caressing him gently. "Lead on, globe trotter, and start me on my first tottering steps."

Hilda Capricorn Fallon sat in a plain straight chair by a flickering fire. Bull sprawled in another chair near her and gazed into the dancing flames. Hilda flinched slightly and unbuttoned her dress. Her stomach bulged in a sizable arc and the skin over it was as smooth as peach down. The flickering rays of the fire played on its amber perfection and Bull laid a rough hand gently on its surface. His eyes opened wide as he put gentle pressure on her. "Well... cus mah cats... feel dat li'l sap-sucker kickin'?" Hilda smiled and put her hand on top of his. "He's been doing that for a couple of days now."

Bull shook his head in amazement. "Whut you kno 'bout dat. Sho is gittin active quick-like."

Hilda smiled and kissed him on an inky cheek. "It's kinda cool. Will you close the window?"

Bull rose to his feet and pulled the swinging window shut.

Outside there stood a great red horse with a shadowy rider. At his heels was a Belgian shepherd dog who watched the lighted square of the house with somber yellow eyes. On the horse's back the girl sat as still as carved stone. Her face was cut with lines of... who could tell? Calipers were around the mouth and the eyes had lines radiating out toward the hairline. The forehead was cut sharply, too, and one might say that the lines represented pain. She sat a while longer, motionless as the animals with her. Two tears started from her eyes and coursed down, finally running into the corners of her mouth. Her shoulders slumped and her head bent till she only had to raise her wrist a little ways to wipe the tears from her face. Then she silently turned the red horse and they slowly walked away from the house where the closed window only showed faintly lighted cracks. She shuddered against the chill of the night and a desperate loneliness which the closing of the window seemed to exemplify. Shut out. Shut out of the warmth of other lives. Shut out of the close comradeship of her fellow man. Her shoulders slumped ever lower and the girl, the horse, and the dog passed on down the hill to be swallowed up in the gloom of night.

THE END